A New era for women: health without drugs

Edward Hooker Dewey

Contents

INTRODUCTION. 7
LECTURE I. 10
LECTURE II. 16
LECTURE III. 21
LECTURE IV. 26
LECTURE V. 32
LECTURE VI. 38
LECTURE VII. 43
LECTURE VIII. 48
LECTURE IX. 53
LECTURE X. 59
LECTURE XI. 63
LECTURE XII. 70
LECTURE XIII. 75
LECTURE XIV. 81
LECTURE XV. 86
LECTURE XVI. 93
LECTURE XVII. 98
LECTURE XVIII. 104
LECTURE XIX. 111
LECTURE XX. 119
LECTURE XXI. 127
LECTURE XXII. 132
LECTURE XXIII. 137
LECTURE XXIV. 144
LECTURE XXV. 152
LECTURE XXVI. 158

A NEW ERA FOR WOMEN: HEALTH WITHOUT DRUGS

BY

Edward Hooker Dewey

INTRODUCTION.

IT is with a spirit of reverence, and a most earnest desire to benefit my sex that I undertake to write the introduction to this wonderful book. It is a volume that means for women all that its title implies, and it opens the way for an immeasurable advance of civilization towards that ideal condition of life which has been promised us, "when man shall have dominion over all things." Therefore is it too much to expect that this "New Era for Women," when read and understood, will receive the recognition it deserves, and will, before the lapse of many years, accomplish in all the fullness anticipated by its enthusiastic author, the disenthralment of womankind from most of those burdens which are now so oppressive, and from which there has seemed heretofore no escape.

The fact that Dr. Dewey is a physician of high standing, having had more than thirty years' experience in the treatment of all kinds of disease, must entitle his utterances to the respectful consideration of the most conservative, startling as such utterances may at first appear; and the additional fact that since the publication of his first book, a little less than a year ago, thousands who have never seen Dr. Dewey are testifying with grateful enthusiasm to the cures wrought by adherence to his teachings, ensures this later work, at the outset, the position and credit to which it is so justly entitled.

As one of the rescued, I can write with all the authority conviction bestows. For several years I suffered with indigestion. To those of my readers who have had a similar experience, and to those only, can that phrase convey its adequate measure of horror. Possessed of a fine constitution, I never succumbed, though the duties of life were to me a weariness inexpressible, and of its pleasures I partook in dreamlike fashion, with no sense of enjoyment, and only a vague wonder at those who had energy enough to even appear happy. I knew that drugs could not cure me, and so I tried, as millions of dyspeptics had done before me, ***dieting,*** with the same discouraging result which generally attends this tedious method of cure. I was almost hopeless of a return to any degree of my former buoyancy and vitality, when I heard of Dr. Dewey's book "The New Gospel of Health," or "The True Science of Living." The title sounded so reassuring that I ordered a copy at once. When it came I was thrilled with hope, as I read Dr. Pentecost's able introduction, for he told of suffering overcome, and of such physical health and mental vigor gained, as he had not hoped would ever again be his. With such a story, from one whose name inspired deep confidence, it is not surprising that I should have read each page that followed, with delight and increasing wonder.

When I had finished the book, which, by the way, was on the very day that I began it, I announced to my family that I was touched by the evident inspiration of the author, and that I believed his statement contained a solution to some of the greatest and some of the most vexatious problems of the day. I further announced that I would never again eat breakfast. Unprepared as they were for such a declaration, they expostulated, and began to offer arguments for health's sake; whereupon I placed the book in their hands, and begged them, for ***health's sake,*** to read it.

My husband, though perfectly well, was so impressed by Dr. Dewey's reasoning that within a week he abandoned the breakfast habit, and since then all the members of our household have been converted.

In the beginning I followed the plan of fasting advised by Dr. Dewey, and at the end of it ate my first meal with all the relish he promised, and with no unpleasant after-effect. During my fast, which extended through four days, I could at intervals have literally devoured a quantity of food, for I had the dyspeptic's appetite; but I had been so particularly imbued with the essence of Dr. Dewey's warning, not to mistake morbid appetite for hunger, that I persevered until there was no mistaking the sensation. My improvement was rapid and continuous, save when I disregarded injunctions, and overate, or indulged a bedtime appetite.

I have written thus fully of myself to encourage those who may need it, and now that is done, I want to say to my readers that it is impossible for those who have not experienced the blessed advantages attendant upon this new method of living to even faintly comprehend them. In no home where breakfast is an established fact can there be the morning harmony and restfulness which exists where breakfast is not.

My personal experience has convinced me that Dr. Dewey has discovered a marvelous physiological truth, which will carry his name down to posterity as one of the greatest benefactors of the human race.

The tendency of the age is toward a lightening of labor in all directions, but in the one in which it is ***most needed, least has been accomplished.*** I refer to the homes all over the world, where the lives of weary women are being ground out by daily routine of work from which a strong man might well shrink appalled. Money, in many instances, cannot help these victims, for money cannot always command efficient service, and in the country and suburban places, often cannot secure even a most indifferent maid of all work. Think then, what Dr. Dewey's message means for us, and breathe a prayer of thankfulness that we live now instead of a hundred years ago, and that the mental attitude of the world is one of such receptivity that it can welcome as a modern Bellerophon this man, who, touched as few have been by the bondage of womankind to ill health and domestic cares, had stepped forward with knightly zeal to smite off the evil heads of a Chimera which has too long, unresisted, preyed upon the strength, the hopes and the lives of the women of all lands.

ALICE MCCLELLAN BIRNEY.
WASHINGTON, D.C.
January, 1896.

LECTURE I.

INTRODUCTORY.

ORIGIN OF THE PRESENT COURSE OF LECTURES—THE PUBLISHER'S CASE NOTED—A VERY SELECT AUDIENCE—HORACE MANN'S DEFINITION OF WOMAN'S SPHERE CONSIDERED—THE HOME MAKER'S ENDLESS TASK CONSIDERED—NATURE AS SEEN BY THE "SAGE OF CONCORD"—POOR HEALTH: ITS EFFECTS ON THE DISPOSITION—WHAT TO BRING TO THE MORNING LECTURES.

My Friends the Women:

A few months ago I had the pleasure of delivering a course of lectures to a little audience of very bright minds on "The True Science of Living," or "The New Gospel of Health." It was essentially the history of a medical evolution, or rather, an evolution of ideas and methods, in the professional care of the sick.

Those lectures had their origin in a series of letters to the President of The Henry Bill Publishing Company, Mr. Chas. C. Haskell, who was in declining health and had been for years, because he had utterly failed to find relief from the remedies and methods of accepted medical science.

He had been admonished to take vacations, and had taken them; had tried all known means and all the list of approved remedies, and yet the slow progress of decline had not been stayed, when one well schooled in the new gospel of health, himself a brand plucked from the burning, sat down before him and opened up words of life to him. Seeing the miracle that had been wrought by the striking contrast with the unsaved man of the years before and quick to see the science behind the miracle, he at once became a willing convert, and for the first time during all his ailing years he began to give his stomach needed vacations. The improvement was so immediate, so striking, that he at once fell in with the idea, that the new method in the cure of disease and in the maintenance of health was worthy to be put in book form. A correspondence ensued, in which the materials for a book were all considered in the form of easily written letters, which only required to be elaborated and styled lectures to fully meet his desires as a publisher.

Those lectures in their published form have been so well received, that there has been an urgent call for a shorter course of lectures to specially meet the peculiar needs of women.

My publisher having lived for more than a year under the "New Gospel" dispensation of health-culture and health maintenance and having regained a degree of mental and physical power not realized since the lusty days of his youth, having seen this new method in life go from one suffering friend to another like a contagion, until thousands are rejoicing over the power of nature to restore the waste places of the body, mind and soul, his urgency that I begin a second series of lectures has at last reached the vehement stage. And so I have invited you especially to listen to this course which I cannot longer delay.

I have invited you especially because of your ready apprehension and keen interest in all that makes human lives better worth living. I have also invited you because you are the best types of the so-called laboring class of your sex. You have all the culture, all the varied, refined, elevated tastes, of your more fortunate sisters of large means in life. There is nothing in art or science, nothing in prose or poetry, nothing in song, or in all nature from atoms to continents, nothing that ever emanates from a human intellect or a human heart that you cannot realize with keenest sense or see with clearest vision, and yet you are living starved lives because of the slavery of toil and undue ailings.

Horace Mann, that prince of American educators of years ago, once said that woman's sphere is a "hemisphere." Ah! ladies, *you* realize every hour how utterly barren that statement is of the merest shade of truth.

A *half* sphere, forsooth? You, by virtue of your heaven-born, quick and endur-ing sympathies, are the only angelic hosts that ever hover over the couches of the sick and dying. Have I not seen this a thousand times? *A half sphere!*

You are your own servants, and all there is in any of your homes worthy of the name is the work of your unaided hands. From cellar to attic, from attic to cellar your duties go on in a ceaseless round, without beginning, without end, day by day, week in, week out, and through all the years of your ability to do and endure; and ever dreaming, ever musing over *what might have* been, *what might* be if some-thing of the ideal *had been, could be attainable.* Yours a half sphere! Perish that word! In all that pertains to human duties performed with endless devotion, in all that requires human sacrifice for human need, the half sphere of woman is a great globe around which the lord of the home revolves as a little satellite. Have I not seen all this with naked eyes, with clearest vision, lo, these many years?

You are yet in the maturity of early womanhood, and yet in every line of your countenances there is an expression of life endured and not enjoyed; there is a sense of "hope deferred" until hopelessness seems to have settled down as a pall over all the outlets of the soul. You go about your daily toil with a gloomy air, with languid movements, with stern duty your taskmaster, your only source of power. With ca-pacities for the highest happiness you are living impoverished, starved lives. Every morning you are compelled to add to the length of your days of toil, by robbing your bodies and souls of that sleep that can only maintain life, and with a pain-ful feeling, that sleep *ends,* must end, because there is no day long enough for the needs of your tasks, it must end where it seems only to have begun.

Why, while I am speaking to you, a lady is under my care who for seven long years has arisen every morning a little after four to get the breakfasts of her husband and son; that is, she has done this every morning when power to do it has not been temporarily lost by illness. I will tell you all about this case later.

You go through your long days with heavy painful steps, and what are your nights when a nervous infant—oh, what suffering has not the wearied mother borne when she could never have a night of unbroken sleep, because of those spells of crying that lacerated the soul as well as the nerves!

I have not been going into homes these many years, by day and by night, to deal with wreckages, without becoming painfully aware of what you do, what you endure and what you suffer!

With what infinite grace of diction did Horace Mann discourse on the "Powers and Duties of Woman," but he had never attended to all the needs of an infant for one week during the first year of its life; had never gotten the 1095 meals of a year, each a little different from every other; had never patched or darned by the hour; had never lamed his back over a washboard, or perspired over a hot flat-iron; had never known what infinite pains the neatness and order of a home ceaselessly demands. Woman's sphere a hemisphere! As a poetic conception it is felicitous in the extreme—but it can only apply to the ideal lives of an ideal world. Ah! ladies, there is no poetry of the spheres in those dull eyes, in the wearied expressions, in those faces of a lifeless tint that are so heavy, so drawn with care.

You came to this first meeting of ours, inhaling the balmy airs of this loveliest of June mornings, but there was little of the Balm of Gilead in it for you. You have walked your ways along as through avenues of Paradise but your wearied eyes have seen little of the matchless tints of many-hued nature. And the air was filled with song but its liquid melody fell only on languid ears. Let me quote from a man who was able to spend his whole life in seeing and telling what he saw:

"In this refulgent summer it has been a luxury to draw the breath of life. The grass grows, the buds burst, the meadow is spotted with fire and gold in the tint of flowers. The air is full of birds, and sweet with the breath of the pine, the Balm of Gilead, and the new hay. Night brings no gloom to the heart with its welcome shade. Through the transparent darkness the stars pour their almost spiritual rays. Man under them seems a young child, and the huge globe a toy. The cool night bathes the world as with a river, and prepares his eyes again for the crimson dawn."

Thus could see, realize and write the "Sage of Concord."

Ladies, there was a great soul in a sound body, and his life's forces had never been stunted by days of taxing labor, or by nights of fitful sleep. "His lines had fallen in pleasant places." All the wealth of scholarship was his, and he went through a long life seeing only the beautiful in literature, the beautiful in nature, and the beautiful and excellent in human character. There was never any grinding between the upper and nether millstone.

Ladies, the grinding has been going on so long in your lives that you are suffering from poor health, which in each of you indicates disease, in a state of development, and sooner or later will suddenly terminate your lives or slowly bring you down to death along the martyr's way. And what are you to do that your lives may have less of bondage and therefore more of leisure, and that you too, may look into "Meadows spotted with fire and gold in the tint of flowers?" Is there any hope where hopelessness has nearly reached the stage of despair? Year by year your duties and cares have multiplied while your powers to meet them have decreased, until duty is no longer a pleasure because it has become a burden, and a burden all the heavier because of your ailings that are presumed to be diseases.

Year by year those attacks of headache have become more frequent and violent, while between attacks, those backs that must bend over the washtub every Monday morning, seem to have been constructed for the special purpose of aching.

Year by year your sense of taste has been getting into a revolt over your own cooking until there are no more meals taken with relish at your own table, and appetite has become a memory except at the table of a friend. For your pains and aches, for your sluggish appetites and stomachs, you have appealed to your family physician and all the patent and recommended remedies in vain. And what about those growing children who are dependent on out-door life for sunshine, because of the danger of stretching lacerated nerves in the house? How many, many times have your souls cried out in anguish over impatient words drawn out as electric sparks, by friction; mourned because you could not be the ever-rested, strong, radiant elder sister, the ready and sympathetic sharer of the gushing joys and noises of younger life! The ideal father, the ideal mother, in addition to being morally and intellectually endowed, always feel well enough to look happy, and hence are never in the electric condition, and they look, act and talk as older children because they *are well.* What power has a genial soul when it is enthroned in a strong body!

I have read that a single hornet has power to break up a camp-meeting, and I believe it. And I have seen fathers and mothers who had become perambulating hornets'-nests with the danger signal always out, because of the electric condition of the nervous system, generated by the frictions of life. The hornet will dart, the spark will fly when the irritation is applied, and moral power rarely avails with restraining force—avails not, because the discharge comes more as a symptom of disease than as the unrestrained outpouring of an unbridled temper, from a naturally defective moral nature.

With this preliminary talk I will dismiss you and I give you this parting, inspiring thought to take with you.

By a change in your living habits there will begin, at this instant, a reversal of the currents of your lives, and all of life's forces shall become busy in the regaining of a great deal of the physical and mental energy and joyousness of soul that was yours when you entered those new homes with such blissful expectations! You will therefore go about the duties, of the day with lighter hearts, and that you may appear before me to-morrow morning with clear heads, you will need to bring empty stomachs into this lecture-room. Why you are to do this will be gradually unfolded during our morning talks. It will be a trying experience for a few mornings, but it will only worry you while you are getting ready for those fresh-air walks—once on the way and all sense of habit-hunger will disappear.

LECTURE II.

LISTENING TO LECTURES WITH EMPTY STOMACHS—REASON AS-SIGNED—STRIKES—NONE IN HOME INDUSTRIES—LONG DAYS AND SHORT NIGHTS—NO CUT IN THE HOURS OF THE HOME-MAKER—DAY-DREAMS OF HEALTH REGAINED AND MAINTAINED BY AUTOMATIC HEALTH-HAB-ITS—GERMS—A NEW SCHEME OF LIVING—ORIGIN AND DEVELOPMENT OF DISEASE—HEREDITARY WEAKNESSES—FIRTS STEPS OF DISEASE THE FIRST LOSS OF THE PHYSIOLOGICAL BALANCE FROM INDIGESTION.

My Friends the Women:

I invited you to appear before me this morning with empty stomachs. The idea was startling to you because for years you have not felt like doing the least thing until some hot drink or a light lunch could relieve the faint, exhausted, all-gone feeling that seemed to hold physical and mental effort in a state of general paraly-sis. You went to your beds last night to dream a little of brighter times to come, and when you arose this morning there was not quite the exhaustion that has been yours for so many years, and the sun, as it arose, seemed for the first time to send its rays within to lighten those chambers of the soul that have been so heavily cur-tained through all the weary years. At first you felt that my admonition could not be carried out, you would faint by the way, or that those violent headaches like an enemy in ambush would pounce upon you; but you were brave, persistent, and so here you are, and are not in a state of general collapse, and though some of you have had hints of the nearness of your ancient enemy, yet there is enough of life left in you to be good listeners to all I shall have to say to you.

The only reason I shall give you, for the present, for appearing before me with empty stomachs is that digestive work always goes on at the expense of mental clearness and physical energy, as you realize every day after you have put your din-ners into the stomachs of your tired bodies, with the resulting stupor that would drive you to your couches but that the taskmaster Duty stands in the way.

You have become my listeners, not only because of your exceeding need, but also because you are so morally and mentally endowed that you will eagerly and instantly catch and absorb every vital truth I shall utter. I need listening powers of the first order that I may attain my needed, highest intellectual reach in giving forth.

To be a discriminating listener, you know, involves rare receptive powers and they are at their best in those who listen as to words of life itself or of death, as we of the medical profession painfully realize, when words of death can only be uttered after all hope has departed.

In these later years a good deal of national history is a history of strikes on the part of men who insist that the hours of toil shall be reduced and the remuneration for each hour shall be increased. In the department of "home industries" there have never been any strikes or any dreams of the possibilities of strikes. You home-makers, you makers of the states and nation have never dreamed that there could be a cut in the hours of your daily toil. For you the hours of the day have been too few and there have not been enough days in the week to meet the exacting demands of your varied, your complex industries. And no human scheme has ever yet been presented whereby your hours and days of toil could be shortened, and your nights of regenerating rest could be lengthened, that you might arise as if born again, with every power charged as with electric force.

Man is ever seeking for a cut in his own hours of toil. No man ever seeks for a cut in those hours that make the rooms of a building his only heaven on earth. Man ever wants a cut in his own hours of toil that he may have more hours of club-life, for down-street sociability, but no man ever sees how your hours can be cut down, and they have been and are very few who have felt your need as they habitually feel their own. And you have had little aid from labor-saving machinery.

In these later years, while your steps have been growing heavier because of the multiplication of your duties and also because of the development of your numerous ailings, ailings that have mocked all remedial efforts, you have sought relief in, or rather have hunted through, various works on health-culture for methods whereby your enfeebled bodies might be trained into power for greater and therefore easier service. But all these have only added life-taxing care to life. You have all found that the growth of the human body into a stronger condition is entirely a work of art, according to the various works of this kind, and not of nature.

There are so many taxing things to be done, taxing in both time and labor; so many things to be avoided, and withal so much thought and care about the health incited, that all methods indicated had to be abandoned. You found that you had neither the time, the strength, nor the patience to become saved on such "plans of salvation." You found only extra work and care, and that was all.

Some of you who are especially endowed with imagination have had your day-dreams; you have dreamed of a life where impaired health might be regained and maintained without the agency of remedies, without any special doing for or thinking about the health. A life void of the fear of disease, which in your eyes has always been your enemy in ambush, ever ready to pounce upon you and lay you low as a "providential dispensation."

What would life be, you have dreamed, if you could have all of your time for your duties and your pleasures by reason of health-habits automatically adjusted, and so adjusted that the greatest possibility of dying only from old age might be reached! And all the more have you so dreamed since our scientists of the microscope are so infesting the air we breathe, the water we drink, and everything we handle with the deadly microbe; why, so infinitely numerous are they said to be that we have never eaten a single meal in all our lives without swallowing millions either alive, roasted or boiled!

And what is kitchen-life to be when the first end of cookery is to get at the exact germ-destroying degree of heat that we swallow only the dead and dying and not the disabled?

And what about the water we drink? Must we needs always have its tasteful qualities boiled out of it and drink it boiling, before it can become again infected? Ah, me! what is life to be while we wait the needed germicides; that is, for all who have strong imaginations?

Now, my friends of the laboring oar, I will make a statement that will rouse all the dull pulses of your weary lives as with an electric charge. I announce to you that I am to present you with a scheme of daily living that will add life to your bodies and souls, that will restore your worn and wasted bodies as the soil of an exhausted farm is restored by a wiser cultivation. I am to offer you a scheme that involves an actual growth towards the normal condition, even as plants grow when the conditions avail; a scheme that involves no study, no thought about what is to be done or not done for the health; that involves no time and labor in method whose good effects are lost when given up, but a scheme that will ***emancipate your lives from one-half of the slavery of your kitchens.***

Well may you look surprised and think it is a very great statement for one very small man to make—and all the more, since such a statement, such a scheme has never before been even hinted at in woman's behalf.

In order that you may better understand how you are to regain your lost health, how your torpid mental and physical energies are to be restored, something about the origin and development of disease is next in order. For if I can make you see very clearly how you have impaired your health, make you see very, very clearly that it has been almost entirely due to avoidable cause, then you will all the more clearly understand how you are to regain your normal condition, and how you are to maintain that normal condition.

Every human being is born with certain structural weaknesses, local or general, due to heredity. These weaknesses are inherent in the single, original cell from which the entire body develops; they determine the exact degree of the constitutional power of the future man or woman, the kind and character of the diseases that may be developed, and even the natural limit of life to the accuracy of a second.

Heredity, then, determines what disease or diseases shall become possible, and violations of the laws of life, avoidable or otherwise, determines when they shall become manifest as developed into the "***attacking*** degree."

Let a hundred persons lie on the cold ground all night, heredity determines what the results shall be, whether pleurisy, pneumonia, rheumatism, etc., and the exposure when it shall be; but the severity, the duration, will be largely a matter of added weaknesses through abuse of the powers of life. Not all would become severely sick by such an exposure, but all would in some way suffer, and they most with the least resisting powers. You may consider, then, that every disease is an inherited possibility, which every violation of the laws of life tends to develop. In this sense, then, pneumonia, pleurisy, rheumatism, etc., is never simply an attack on a well person, but rather a summing up of the results of the more or less lifelong violations of health laws. Here you may ask what is health? The answer is that it is that condition of the body when digestion is so perfect that the physiological balance between the destruction and construction, that goes on ceaselessly in cell-life, is kept duly normal.

The first step, then, in every disease, is loss in digestive power. With a life so perfect that the physiological balance would never be lost, then death would reach the natural limit to a second, and whether at the end of one hour or of one hundred years of existence. Our human lives are very much like bank deposits, to which we can never add a single farthing, and upon which we are entirely dependent for all the needs of our lives; we ought to live on the interest; we generally so draw on the principal that the bankruptcy of death is likely to be invited years before the deposit would be removed by the hand of nature herself.

My friends, on this one subject of the development of disease through avoidable violations of health laws, how the habitual violation of those laws invites, cultivates, develops debility, disease, and how disease may be relieved by a culture in reverse, on ***this*** subject I could speak for days with a holy fervor of conviction, and then the half would not be told you. Little by little, step by step, we hope to find the better life by a better living, by a larger obedience to the divine law of the flesh.

LECTURE III.

THE NEW GOSPEL OF HEALTH—VICTOR HUGO'S DEFINITION OF NAPOLEON APPLIED TO DISEASE—DIPHTHERIA, ANTI-TOXIN; DASHED HOPES—DISEASE A SUMMING UP—A STRIKE NOT AN ATTACK—EVERY DISEASE A CONSTITUTIONAL POSSIBILITY FROM THE GERM-PERIOD OF EXISTENCE—ITS ADVANCE ALONG LINES OF LEAST RESISTANCE—POINTS IN ITS AVOIDABLE CULTURE INDICATED—GOOD HEALTH DEFINED—A MOST SURPRISING FACT IN NATURE ANNOUNCED—THE BRAIN, THE POWER-HOUSE OF THE HUMAN PLANT, HAS A POWER OF SELF-NOUR-ISHMENT IN TIME OF SICKNESS—IT ACTUALLY EATS THE LEAST IMPOR-TANT TISSUES OF THE BODY WHEN THERE IS NO DIGESTION OF FOOD—SEVERAL POINTS IN SUPPORT OFFERED—WHY THE SICK SHOULD NOT BE FED.

My Friends the Women:

The scheme of living to which I have invited your consideration is styled "The New Gospel of Health," by my publisher. He found such immediate benefit by the adoption of its methods and the science involved was so readily comprehended, that straightway he began to preach it to his martyr friends. Being a man of large business affairs, the idea that he could regain his health by methods that did not involve the cost of any time, nor the least taxing of his brain, struck him as being a gospel of good news to the afflicted that ought to be sent to the ends of the earth. And why should he not so feel and act, when for more than a year and a half the lost powers and energies of youth seemed to have been fully regained, and who has seen his gospel go from friend to friend until thousands are rejoicing who were travelling along the martyr's way to premature graves?

He has found, as all his friends have found, that it is not a salvation by grace but a saving of life by a larger avoidance of causes that lead to death; or by a closer walk with God according to laws "manifest in the flesh."

Victor Hugo has termed Napoleon "A mysterious something that gazes like an eagle and strikes like a thunderbolt." Very much in this light is disease considered by the masses, and generally by the profession. It is always a mystery, a dread possibility, in the life of every human being, and one only to be dealt with by the mystic methods of drugs. Only one short year ago the entire medical world (except a few hard-headed skeptics) and all the people were waiting with bated breath, with intense hope, and largest expectation, that at last an antidote had been found for that destroyer of homes, diphtheria. One short year, and what hopes have been dashed and how great has been the fall of Anti-toxin!

My friends, if there be one thing that I must insist upon more than any other, that I must dwell upon and put down before you, line upon line, must repeat over and over again, and yet once again, it is this one idea in particular, that disease is never an attack, but always a *summing up,* that it is one of Nature's strikes from long endured and largely avoidable abuse of the laws of life that may be easily apprehended, and therefore not to be dealt with by specifics administered through a hollow needle, with any reasonable expectations of cure, reasonable from the standpoint of cause and effect, as viewed by a scientist. And, mark my words, you must always be on the defence against not only that destroyer of homes, diphtheria, but against all other diseases and ailings.

Nature's strikes like the strikes in business are always destructive and always will be, and they need not specifics in their convulsive throes but specific avoidance of operative causes, and since you and I are not to live long enough to see disease successfully treated by the miracle of germ-antidotes, which really involves the idea of an easy pardon for the cumulative results an violated laws, does it not become us to know all we can of the knowable, as to the origin and development of disease? Will it not be very much better for us to believe that these strikes of nature can be prevented even as the strikes of business, by a rational dealing with causes and not hope in vain for the undiscovered germ-killer?

What would it not, will it not, be worth to you to believe that for your own lives behind the lives of those children, there is no frowning Providence? What will it not be worth to you that your own life is largely in your own keeping, and that there is no Providence ever ready by an afflictive dispensation to torture your lives up to a higher plane of spiritual living, by torturing their lives out of earthly existence? Oh! the virtues of the "chastening rod" when its meaning is never truly interpreted!

In order that there shall be something of method in laying out and unfolding this new "plan of salvation," this "New Gospel of Health," "This True Science of Living," I will enumerate some of its vital points in order:

(1) Every disease that has ever afflicted mortal man or woman or child was a constitutional possibility from the germ-state of existence. This has already been asserted.

(2) The first step in every disease is the first loss of digestive power, or the first decline of this power, no matter how slight.

(3) Disease advances along the lines of the least resistance, the resisting power in all cases, originally, being the exact measure of the power inherent in heredity. As the weak link is the exact measure of the strength of the chain, so are the parts structurally weak through heredity the exact measure of a human body to resist the advances of disease.

(4) Whatever lowers digestive power is always the first, direct exciting cause of disease. No matter how slight this may be, its greatest influence is felt on constitutionally weak structures. They are seemingly points of attack, as the weak points in the enemy's lines are the points aimed at by the attacking army.

(5) Every morsel of food that gets into a human stomach beyond the power to digest and assimilate is always the direct, the exciting cause of disease; it is always one of the links, that, link by link, added day by day, sooner or later ends in the

mysterious "attack," the "providential dispensation."

This is a startling statement, for it involves the idea that there is a great deal of suicide in these human lives of ours, and it is no less startling than true.

I have already given you a definition of health. I will now give you one of good health, or rather tell you what that condition means to the individual. Have you ever seen a horse when he "paweth in the valley and rejoiceth in his strength"? *There,* is ***strength, health, power, in reserve.*** How such a condition mocks at disease and the pestiferous bacillus! All this is a memory with you, but you see it in the nursery, in the play-ground, in the school-yard.

Habitually perfect digestion of all food eaten means habitually perfect health, and all the strength and endurance, all the reserves of mental and physical power, the constitutional idea through heredity makes possible. Anything less than this means a decline in the reserves and advance in disease. I tell you, and with all the emphasis that human words can express, that on the question of ***what*** affects digestive power, ***how*** surplus food by the tax it costs vital power to dispose of it, ***invites, cultivates,*** and ***develops disease, all the world, including the medical profession, is in a state of profound sleep.*** How this is I will make you see clearly later.

(6) Now for a genuine surprise, for I have one of the most wonderful facts in all nature to unfold to you, to my mind the most wonderful that pertains to these bodies of ours. You are all aware that the brain is the power-house of the human plant; that it is the source of all physical, mental and moral energy. Would you not think, then, that an organ so all-important would need extraordinary provisions for its continuous safety? Certainly, and hence the skull of flinty hardness to enclose and shield from the injury of accident. But this is not all, this wonderful structure, the brain, has power to ***feed itself for days and weeks when no food is being digested, and how?***

You are all aware that in time of sickness the body constantly loses weight until the natural appetite is regained, even though food is being taken the while;

this being the fact would it not naturally seem reasonable to a reasonable person, that it is not being digested and assimilated, and hence doing no good whatever? It strikes me very much in that way. Well, now, what is becoming of those wasting tissues, or rather disappearing tissues, for they are not wasting? Of course you have never given this always clearly manifest fact a single thought. Let me tell you. The brain ***actually eats them up,*** and right along during every second of the enforced fast of the sickness. Is not this wonderful? And see how reasonable this brain is, in the choice of its food. It actually seems to prefer fatty tissue, which of all tissues we can spare with the least inconvenience, and with the least loss of strength, and get back most readily when we get to eating again.

Now, this fact that the brain loses no weight in sickness or even when death comes from starvation, has been known to physiologists I doesn't know how long. But that the fat, the skin and the muscles, for the brain, too, is dainty and prefers a varied bill of fare, that these and other easily spared tissues are actually brain food and the only food that it can appropriate during the absence of digestive power, is a fact that has never been apprehended by the medical profession in any practical sense. Hence, all over the world the hapless sick are compelled to eat whether or no, and ***by so much is nature handicapped while warring with disease.***

As this wonder of nature is entirely new to you, I will enumerate some of the important evidences in its support:

(a) In all post-mortems, no matter how wasted the body, the brain is found to fill the cranial cavity when not itself diseased.

(b) The mind is often clear to the last moment of life, even when the body has become emaciated to the skeleton degree. This could not be if the brain had become emaciated.

(c) The tissues do disappear during sickness, and what becomes of them if they are not used to feed the brain, and perhaps also the heart and lungs, for these never reveal any appreciable loss during disease when they themselves are not diseased?

(d) For eighteen years, while in continuous attendance on the acutely sick, I have in every case permitted the brain to feed itself in its own way, and in not a single case, where death was not beyond all question inevitable, did it fail to do it-self ample justice and in some cases for four, five, six weeks, and even longer.

(e) And in strong support of the conception of this wonderful power of the brain has been the fact that, as disease declined, mental, moral and physical energy increased. What better feeding of the sick can a rational, human being ask for, than the feeding that nature prescribes, and that it should be such, it has placed a sentinel at the danger-point in the garb of a food-loather, to shield the reparative processes while the battle with disease is going on?

Aversion to food is the sleepless, tireless sentinel, ever on the guard lest the enemy gets into the stomach while the battle with disease is going on.

I will now let you go to your homes to think over these points I have enumerated, and especially the last because of its exceeding interest, but also because of its importance, as a matter of vital need and of the largest practicality in the care of the sick.

LECTURE IV.

"NO-BREAKFAST" PLAN OF LIVING—NOT GIVEN UP BUT POST-PONED—ITS ORIGIN AS A PLAN OF DAILY LIVING—OPPOSITION—WHY GIVEN UP—MORNING HUNGER MORBID WANT, A DISEASE IN PROCESS OF CULTURE—A BANKER'S STATEMENT—WHY GO WITHOUT YOUR BREAKFAST?—REST, SLEEP, DOES NOT CAUSE HUNGER—ABILITY TO LA-BOR WITH THE STOMACH EMPTY—A CUT IN THE HOME-MAKER'S HOURS OF LABOR A STRIKING ILLUSTRATION.

My Friends the Women:

The very first thing in this higher life I am to tell you about involves the loss of your breakfast. It has been called the "no breakfast plan of living." In the ordinary sense that is true but not in the etymological sense, as the first meal of the day must be the break of the fast, regardless of the time of the day when it is taken.

In the sense I will have you understand it, it involves a postponement of your first meal to a much later time than has been your lifelong custom. Now if there is one meal that has been considered the meal of meals throughout all America, to impart strength for the toils of the day, it has been the early morning meal. With most toilers, whether the brain or the muscle, there is always in some degree a sense of exhaustion on arising, such as would seem in a physiological sense to be induced by exhaustive exercise mental or physical. This has always been assumed to indicate the need of food to impart power to life's forces, even as the fire-box of the engine needs coal to raise mechanical force.

When some twelve years ago or more the citizens of Meadville, Pa., became aware that one of their established physicians was actually advising some of his patients to fast until the midday meal, opinion became very emphatic but was somewhat divided,—but really *opinion* is not the term I need in this case, for it was not a matter of opinion at all, but rather of *absolute belief* or *knowledge.* About half of the citizens (except my own patrons), *knew* the idea was founded on *idiocy,* and the other *knew* that it was founded on *lunacy.* From thence I became and remained a marked man, the originator and promoter of a heresy believed, nay, *known* to be absolutely dangerous to life, and all the more as it had reached the public ear that my patients who died went down to death with the pangs of hunger added to the pangs of disease.

The novelty of the idea attracted all the more attention because it had originated and was being vigorously pushed by a *physician* who, by virtue of his professional education and experience, must have become demented or a lunatic to be guilty of taking away the most important meal of the day as a *curative agency* in the treatment of *disease.*

Even with the most conservative minds the idea seemed to be void of sense or science or of the least practicality, hence, self-evidently wrong. Only a few days ago one who feels that he has entered upon a new lease of life by way of this method of living, went into the office of one of the most distinguished lawyers in the state of Pennsylvania, and chanced to speak of his new ways of living, and that a book had been written upon the subject by his physician. Now this great legal light had often gone before juries and begged them to see with microscopic vision, with philosophic application, every scintilla of evidence he had adroitly extracted from his witness and then bring in the verdict for his client; but on this matter he only needed to *hear,* to *know* immediately, that the physician who advises people to go without breakfast is a *fool*—he could, in such a case, at once know, without evidence, and had never once thought, that not only the very first meal but the very last meal that a human being takes is a breakfast, as well as all the other meals.

Now, as each one of you, living in a different community, and where the idea is to be known for the first time, are to meet with the usual opposition, I may as well forecast the fact that this opposition will be only the natural sensitiveness to light, of eyes accustomed to darkness, that the more violent the opposition the more dense the darkness, and when, in the course of time, you have become so illumined by the light of the science there is behind every method advised, and are rejoicing over the powers of youth again realized on earth, you will often wonder, will often ask, "Why do the heathen rage and imagine a vain thing?" and will wonder that "they will not come that they might have life."

You henceforth are not only to realize better, healthier and more leisurely lives, but you are to become evangelists to all your suffering friends, and your light will be so placed that it shall be seen by all with whom you come in contact; but your lives are to become involved in more or less of conflict with the unenlightened minds about you, for though the spread of this "New Gospel of Health" is a ministry of instruction and of enlightenment, it meets the opposition of ignorance as to its having a basis of science.

With me it was for many, years a ministry of self-sacrifice, not only in the notoriety of being held up as the crank-in-chief of an entire city but in the business sacrifice it involved, in that it was believed that my attendance on the sick was the certainty of having the danger of starvation added to the danger of disease, and hence my services were a danger that needed to be ***guarded against*** by warnings couched in every form of language.

You are to be opposed in the adoption of this new method in life, not only in your own homes but within the entire sphere of your social life. The home-opposition will decline as it is seen that so far from there being any disabling results realized, there will instead be a positive gain in a general awakening of all your powers, that can be seen by all with "naked eyes," and hence all protests, will be merged into silent acquiescence, and in due time the entire household will be in line with you.

Said a prominent banker to me, recently: "Doctor, myself, wife, servant-girl and dog are living on two daily meals." And so the "cult" spreads through entire families. I will here suggest to you who are fond of a little intellectual fencing that there is no little pleasure in meeting obdurate skeptics on all the new lines of life, because they are all in ***accord with physiological law*** and hence are ***unanswerable,*** as the great lawyer soon found out when the science was unfolded to him.

You are now well ready to consider with the keenest interest and in all its bearings this great question: "What is there in this new scheme of living for women in all her relations in life?" In other words, you may ask, "What have you been doing for women in your own city to give them healthier, more leisurely, and therefore more cheerful, lives? And how permanent are the results in this way?" You shall all know.

And now to begin at the beginning, to begin with the first step, why go without the breakfasts? You have all done so now for four mornings and for the special purpose of mental clearness. You were quick to see that this would be the result when you recalled the mental and physical sluggishness always felt after a hearty meal is taken. You feared, however, that you would get so faint that you would not be able to listen, and as far as those headaches were concerned, they would be certain as a result, but you found that you were stronger by far than you expected, and that in the excitement of listening to the lectures your head seemed to forget to ache.

Were I to ask what the best preparation would be for a day of hard physical toil, your answer would at once be, a long night of perfect sleep, which is only another name for perfect rest. Well, then, at the end of such a night there ought to be a perfectly rested condition, and if perfectly rested, you are certainly perfectly ready to begin your day of toil. Having been in a state of rest during all the hours of the night, can you be, ought you to be, hungry on arising? You never thought of this in this way before. You can very clearly see what the need of food is to one who has been engaged all the forenoon in the heaviest manual labor of a January day, but you cannot see how perfect sleep, perfect rest, can make you hungry. Nor can any one else see how it should be.

Morning hunger, so-called, is morbid want, arising always from a life-long habit of eating before the need has appeared, and it is a want that indicates, not the need of food, *but actual disease* in the process of development. Now there are very few people who have such a feeling of hunger in the morning that they eat with any pleasure; hence, always, the eating is done to satisfy the morbid want, or rather complaint of nature, and with the shopmen and others who have their forenoons employed, food is also taken to forestall a case of hunger before the time of the next regular meal; hence the stomach is made a vehicle to carry food about for several hours before it can possibly be needed.

Morning hunger then, I repeat, is not real hunger, but disease in course of development, and the more sharp it is, the louder it is as a *danger signal.* How do I know this, you ask? First, for the reason, as I have stated, that sleep *never, never* makes you hungry; and second, because of the thousands who have given up the morning meal of life-long continuance, all want of it has been found to totally disappear. Now can you think for one moment, that if you actually need this early meal, nature would let you off so easily? No indeed, she will never be satisfied with less than her needs without discomforting protests. She will always complain when the books are not kept duly balanced.

Now let me assure you, that of the thousands who have given up the early meal they have not only lost all want of it, but have found that they can labor with muscle or mind for several hours with more energy and spirit before hunger comes than they ever had when using their stomachs as morning lunch-pails.

In this line of experience the evidence is all one way, and it is **unquestionable** that after a night's restful sleep, it actually requires several hours of heavy manual labor to develop **natural hunger.** Now, my listening friends, you slaves of needless labor in your kitchens, cannot you see a great light looming right up before you in a cut of your hours of labor? Can it be otherwise, if not one of the members of your family can by any possible severity of the forenoon-toil get so hungry as to need a morsel of food until near the time of the usual second meal of the day? What will it not be worth to you to have one-third of your kitchen work abolished at one "swoop"? **Ideal,** is this? Not at all; it is a matter of instant practicability. Let me give you an example. One winter forenoon I was called to a family where the mother was doing the work for husband, self and six children, one an infant. That was all the work that just one woman could possibly do. It was hers to get up every morning of the week an hour before the others, to get a general breakfast, including ham, sausage or steaks, etc.; and when, after an hour before the stove, then there would be the fraction of an hour to inhale the smoke of griddle-cakes. And all this for a family that had had no exercise except in dressing. Need I tell you that when the last dish was put away, this enslaved woman was not only tired enough for some hours of rest, hut also that it was about time to begin to get the next general meal?

Said I to this cheerless woman, "Would you like to know how to keep me out of your house and so save doctor's bills?" "Indeed I would, Doctor." And the dull features were at once ablaze with curious interest. Well then, I will tell you just how it can be done. To-morrow morning you lie in bed until it is time to have those children dressed for breakfast, and then invite them to break their fast on just bread buttered, with some warm drink. As it was a German family, and strong coffee had been the usual morning drink, I suggested water, only flavored with coffee as a compromise substitute. Now it cost about five minutes to get such a breakfast and about ten to clean away all after it; and though there were noisy protests at the limited bill of fare at first, perfect reconciliation soon came.

Now there were in this instance the needless hours of labor saved in the morning, and every day in the week keen hunger for the plainer foods, the desire for pastries and fancy dishes being very much diminished. So much saved then in the morning hours, with the added pleasure of being able to get the dinner without fatigue, and with the certainty that it would be keenly relished. The dinners became simpler than before, and another great point gained was in much more thorough digestion, by reason of the lighter morning meal; and hence, in due time, the evening meal was very much simplified.

Now this woman has been testing this plan for nearly four years, and I have been in the house only on two occasions since to advise for trivial ailings. With her kitchen-work cut down, and the highest average health realized, there has been one of the most grateful of all women for services rendered. You at once see that on my part, the moral far exceeds the business consideration in such professional services, and yet such has been the agitation in my native city over what seems to be the "starving method" in the treatment of human ailings, that every man or woman, not enlightened, would have advised with honest conviction, that of all medical advices available to this woman, mine should be avoided as absolutely dangerous to even life itself. Now when I tell you that since our last meeting I have seen this woman and have been told that she is now doing all the work of a family of nine, and that the dinner so well satisfies that the evening meal has become the lightest of prepared table-meals, that she knows that her kitchen work has been cut down more than one-half, *you* can go to your homes full of hope for the future.

LECTURE V.

BRAIN-FEEDING FURTHER CONSIDERED—FEEDING THE SICK—Is AVERSION TO FOOD IN TIME OF SICKNESS ONE OF NATURE'S GRAVE MISTAKES?—A DEFENSE OF DAME NATURE—GENERAL REASONS WHY THE SICK CANNOT DIGEST FOOD, POINTED OUT—THEIR IMPORTANCE—

THE CURE OF DISEASE NATURE'S OWN WORK—THE TRUE PHYSICIAN A GUARD—AN INTERPRETER—AN ILLUSTRATION—A VERY PERTINENT QUESTION ASKED AND ANSWERED—A DECEIVED PHYSICIAN.

My Friends the Women:

In all your lives you have never had apprehension so keen, so agonizing, as when you have been hovering over those couches, and seeing with keen vision the bodies of those sick children wasting away and unable to supply by feeding, all you sorely felt they needed.

You have never in all your lives had so much as the slightest suggestion occur to you that feeding never, never arrests the waste when enforced flatly against nature's will. Nor has it occurred to your family physicians. The one all-abounding idea in all cases is, that vital power, or the strength, must be supported while the conflict with disease is on.

This supposed need of vital support, great with the gravity of disease would seem to make the aversion to food a serious mistake on the part of nature, or a serious mistake on the part of the physician who enforces food.

I will now enter upon a defense of the good dame for her persistent warning against physicians and anxious, agonized friends for this apparently dangerous eccentricity of aversion to food when of all times eating seems to be the supremest necessity, and defend her on the line of adverse digestive conditions.

It will not be denied by any intelligent person that for the perfect digestion of a meal there must not only be the keen relish, hunger only incites, but there must also be perfect health and the loftiest cheer of mind. Cheer is as the draft to the fire in its effect on digestive energy. In order that you may better understand the matter from the standpoint of nature, I will enumerate her chief objections to enforced food in time of sickness; the fact that for brain reasons it is not in the least necessary, being naturally and easily first. Sickness, as you all know, is a reversion of all health habits and by so much of digestive conditions.

(1) A furred tongue and a loss of the sense of relish.

(2) The mouth and stomach abnormally dry, hence loss of digestive fluids.

(3) Mental depression.

(4) Loss of muscle and nerve energy, hence food is not made to revolve about the stomach as in health.

(5) The prone position interfering with the circular sweep of the food about the stomach as takes place in the erect posture.

(6) Confinement in rooms with the air more or less fixed, very much more so than ever occurs in health.

(7) Absence of general muscular activity, always the most rapid promoter of hunger, of digestive conditions.

(8) Pain, and even the slightest sense of discomfort having their relative effect as digestive depressors.

(9) Loss due to imperfect sleep.

In line with these points is the fact that no one will question, that there is never any sense of refreshment when food is taken without hunger; there never fails to be a sense of refreshment when food is taken **with** hunger. Now with the brain abundantly capable of feeding itself so long as any feeding can avail, always able to fully care for itself in this way and absolutely free from the adverse conditions to stomach digestion, always fully able to feed itself during the period of aversion to food in all cases where death is not inevitable, what think you of the enforced feeding of the sick? And in particular if it be true that, as symptoms decline, the strength we are always so anxious to support, ***actually increases*** without the least feeding, without any of our meddling, depressing interference?

Another very important point I will call your attention to, and that is that the cure of any and all diseases is solely the work of the divine hand of nature, even as is the cure of the fractured bone or of the amputated limb; there is no science in dosage, because there can be no need of doses in the mere matter of those reconstructive changes in cell-life that go on, that must go on in the cure of disease; as well think these processes need drugs as the processes by which the body was originally developed. For the cure of disease nature requires very little at our hands; so much is this the fact, that there are only the half dozen or so of relieving doses that ever avail for good in any case of sickness.

My friends, will it be worth anything to you in any sad times to come as you hover over those couches to believe that you ***know*** that in all cases where death is not inevitable, nature will do all the curing and with no enforced food, with few if any remedies, and if your heavy, disturbing hands are kept aloof it will be all the more well and rapidly done?

The several points I have now given you constitute the foundation of the course of morning talks I am to give you. They are the several strings upon which I must play a limited number of tunes with such variations as their character will admit. If there shall be a great deal of sameness, of repetition, of undue enthusiasm, it will be because of my profound impression that they are nature's own points, and of your exceeding need to know them. But here comes a question from one of you.

"Doctor,—What are our physicians to do for our sick, if these most intensely interesting points are true, and as you state them they seem self-evident, if nature does all the curing and with little if any drugs? Are we to no more need our trusted family physicians, and are we to trust nature alone, hereafter, in our times of trial? Or are we and ours to be no more sick?"

Signed, "The Deeply Interested."

In reply to this very pertinent question the answer is, that by reason of ancestral weaknesses and the unavoidable adverse conditions to health that is the experience of every human being, sicknesses more or less severe, are the possibilities, the probabilities of all, and when these shall come you will need your trusted physician as before, to lean upon, to stand by, as nature's guard, as nature's interpreter for ***your need.*** As a guard do you say? You scarcely realize how much a guard a physician is even as a check to the thoughtless proffers of aid that are inevitable from the tender-hearted sympathetic friends, whose impulses are the noblest that can stir the human heart. Why, there is yet a woman under my care who has a severe bowel trouble, and yet in my absence the kind neighbor called and insisted that she must drink milk several times a day, boiled with suet, ***suet!!*** Only just think, a sick ***stomach*** and ***sick bowels,*** and several meals daily of whey, tallowed ***cheese, curds, swallowed whole!!!*** Certainly there was variety in that bill of fare and a need to defend against it.

A few weeks ago in a case of intense bowel trouble in a young girl, and with no trained and trusty nurse to guard in my absence, the kind neighbor, with the noblest of human motives, did go in and get a dose of castor-oil into that stomach that would not retain water, with such alarming results as to seem to endanger life for a time. Never having been engaged in the practice of medicine, you have no idea of how much the sick need guarding from the frenzied proffers of encumbering help. No, you will always need your physicians to interpret, to lean upon, and especially to guard against unprofessional aid. But in the times to come there will be a decline in the need of the mere matter of dosage as the superstition of the materia medica gives way to a deeper insight into the divine law of healing.

This course of lectures is not to make you your own family physicians, but to cut down your need of them by teaching you those ways that lead to life and not to disease and death.

Another question.

"Doctor,—What are we to do hereafter when our physicians insist we must feed our sick in order to keep up the strength?"

Signed, "Anxious Listeners."

This also is very pertinent as well as a very direct question. And my answer is, that if what I have given you in the several points be true, and you believe it to be true, then you can enforce the feeding with very feeble hands and realize no rasping of conscience thereby, and you may be assured that your sick will not suffer loss because you have suffered a very marked decline of your coaxing powers. In this city a very intelligent lady had an attack of pneumonia, with her family physician a heavy doser and feeder. By a confidential arrangement with her nurse her doctor was permitted to make his daily visits, and to change his dosing as he saw the need, but never a dose was taken or any food. In due time, when all the symptoms were allayed and the appetite for food had come, she asked him this very pertinent, this very ***direct question:*** "Doctor, as you have had other similar cases during my sickness, how have I got along as compared with the others?" And the answer was, "***the best of any!***"

Why should she not have done the best when the curing had to be done solely by nature, and there had been no taxing of vital power in getting rid of decomposing food, and the stomach had been permitted the rest nature designed it should have? No, when you are admonished that you must feed your sick, recall all these points, and then let your fight against nature be a sham one; make a show of effort to get by the guarded gate of taste, and if you fail, nature will bend low before you, not to plead, not to beg for more, unless it be for more sham in the effort.

Now that you have gotten your attention called to the fact that only nature cures and that the brain can feed itself, you will become apt scholars, and the more you observe the more you will believe.

And as you get your minds more and more enlightened, you will not hold your physicians to such unreasonable accountability in the adjustment of remedies to the supposed needs of nature, in her efforts to reconstruct the wrecked bodies of the sick.

The several points or basal facts I have given you, I hope I have given with such force that they will stick until they germinate, to henceforward be a part of your "stock in trade" as vitalized knowledge. We always understand that most readily that seems to be most vital to our needs, and retain it longest. As I shall have nothing to impart to you that I shall not think vital to the higher lives that you are to live, I shall try to make you so understand that you will not require the aid of note-books in the processes of vitalization.

LECTURE VI.

EVIDENCE OF IMPROVED NUTRITION OBSERVED IN THE LISTENERS— AN EARLY MORNING MEAL PERMITTED AND CONSIDERED, BUT NOT AD-VISED—TWO MEALS A DAY FOR GROWING CHILDREN—EVOLUTION OF DIGESTIVE POWER—EMPTY STOMACHS AND FORENOON PHYSICAL AND MENTAL STRENGTH—A CUT IN THE HOURS OF KITCHEN LABOR—AN IN-SPIRING OUTLOOK.

My Friends the Women:

I begin the talk of this morning with the suggestion that my eyes have become exceedingly keen for seeing the evidences of the better nutrition of the body, both with eyes that see without, and those that see within, and already I see brighter and brightening eyes; I see the hints of color in your faces while every line of expression seems to be rousing with "newness of life." All this is very cheering to me, for no husbandman has ever had keener eyes for color, and for all evidences of a vigorous growth in those crops whereof he is to live and not starve, than I have for the evidences of growth in a starved human body with its starved soul. Every morning I shall detect evidences of growth in the deepening of the tints, in the energy and cheer of the expression, and in the easier grace and force of all your movements. You have already found for lecture-room purposes that you have had no need to use your stomachs as lunch carriers. But here comes a question to be answered.

"Doctor,—In the case of the family you told us about in your last lecture it seems that you permitted all of them to eat immediately after dressing; how does this accord with your teaching?"

Signed, "Anxious Mother."

I am very glad to consider this very pertinent question. Had I begun at first to advise no eating in the morning, I think that even my best friends would have had serious doubts as to my sanity. Human progress, human progression, is a matter of steps and inches, a creeping for a time with an uncertain gait. Had I advised no breakfast in that family, it would not have been even for one moment considered, the light would have been too, too strong for unaccustomed eyes, and then what a war of defense she would have had against all the powers of darkness from without; for you of the gentler sex not only have quicker, more intense sympathies, but also convictions of red-hot fervency, and a seeming starvation of a whole family of innocent children would have invited protests unceasing.

You easily see then, that I had to adjust the light to the receptive power of the eyes. "But Doctor, would you advise that growing children should habitually go without their breakfasts, or the early morning meal as you would have it?" Certainly, and because they are growing. If you inhale even a single breath of a sleeping child or youth in the morning, as a general fact, you will be moved to inhale your next breath from an open window, and because the tired stomach of the tired body was not equal to surplus food during all the hours of the night, hence you get an odor from a food mass in a state of decomposition. Now on arising, it will require several hours of fresh-air exercise, to complete the overtask of the night and to get the stomach well in line for the duties of a much relished meal later on.

"But do you really think Doctor, that growing children would do as well on two, as upon three meals a day?" Certainly if their meals are regulated by the time of hunger and not by the time of day. No child ever lived or ever will live, that has had or can have either the need, or the ability, to thoroughly digest more than two general meals *in one day.* No child ever lived that would not have eaten more meals per year when eating only two meals per day, than when trying to eat three meals per day. This is easily accounted for by the better average health, by which days and weeks of eating are not lost, through headaches, bilious attacks, colds, etc.

I am now ready to make, and you to hear, this most emphatic statement, that it is the usual experience of those who have given the no-breakfast idea the fairest and longest test, that the forenoon is the best half of the day for heavy labor, whether in wielding the pen or *swinging the scythe or the ax!!* Theoretically this ought to be so; practically, in every kind of human labor, thousands have proven it to be so to their entire satisfaction.

This statement would seem to become self-evident, when I recall the fact that digestive energy means a loss of physical and mental energy, and that the brain keeps itself duly nourished during all the hours of the morning fast that ends with hunger, relieved by the keenly-relished food. Do you believe it, can you but believe it? It is a law of God, manifest in human flesh, eternal as the rock-ribbed mountains, and no balanced human intellect, in or out of the profession will care, or even dare, to abate one shade from its tremendous meaning in all that pertains to the well-being of the human body, of the human intellect and of the human soul.

Now let me take another step in advance. The next thing to stating a fact is the reason for its existence. You now are thoroughly convinced that neither your-selves, your children, nor any of your suffering friends, who for a time, will almost violently oppose this higher Christianity in living, have even the least need of food at the ordinary breakfast hour. What are the conditions of the digestive organs on arising after a night of sleep? The answer is, must be, a complete absence as there ought to be, of digestive conditions; the little glands of the stomach are as the cow's udder after the morning milking, empty and probably in a state of absolute repose. But as the mental and physical machinery gets into continuous activity, so do these glands of the stomach during each moment of the fast that should be ended when hunger comes, so do they develop power, as do also those of the mouth to throw out their dissolving floods, into such food as hunger only ever invites to the digestive process.

Can any enlightened, balanced intellect *in* the profession deny, that this is the inevitable, physiological result of a morning or any other fast that continues until hunger comes? Can any deny that any human mouth ever waters except the mouth of *hunger?* Deny therefore that any human stomach is ever able to throw out its waters of life except the stomach of hunger? Gentlemen and ladies of the medical profession, why is it that you do not see the utter futility of the enforced feeding of the sick; nay more, why is it that you do not see that it is *war against nature, dangerous disproportion to the gravity of the disease?*

You now see as you never saw before that a human stomach, even as a cow's udder, must have some *undisturbed hours,* if there are any dissolving floods to be poured out. But there is another very important development, the nerve; the sense of taste also gains in functional power that supreme sense, through which nature is able to ask for just the kinds of food she needs to restore her waste places, and also by which eating becomes one of the most acutely pleasurable of all human experiences. Is this deniable? Can any one deny this?

I can easily see, my enslaved friends of the kitchen, as these inspiring physiological facts become more and more your own, and the need of the taxing breakfasts fades away, that there is a brighter glisten to your eyes, for you begin to see a tremendous cut in your hours of labor, and more hours of that sleep that shall make your earth, that now is, more like your heaven that is to be.

Ah you women of the laboring class, you home-makers, makers of states and nations, the only heaven that you have ever looked forward to has been a heaven, not of eternal sleep, but of *eternal rest,* a heaven where there are no enforced physical activities, where there are no long weary days and long faces! Your *heavenly heights* have always been directly above your *kitchenly depths,* with the *space between infinite!*

Well may your eyes begin to brighten as it dawns upon you that emancipation of one-third of your time in those lowest depths has become a certainty beyond all question. A cut of one-third is a great deal, as you easily believe. Now let us see if the remaining two-thirds cannot be so reduced as to somewhat resemble in outline one-half. I am able to announce to you that in all families where all eating has been given up until after several hours of the usual morning activities, the always relished first meal is so thoroughly digested as to make the second meal a matter of very minor importance as to variety and character, and is often skipped, without the least disabling result on the following morning's ability to labor with brawn or brain.

Now does not one general meal and one light one equal about one-half of three whole ones in the time and labor spent in their preparation? There are the figures that "do not lie," and another very important feature, a feature of keen interest from your own standpoint, is the habitual fact that those meals are taken with such relish that there will be heard very little criticism. O woman! how often has your soul been lacerated, because you failed to so flavor those meals that feeders who were not hungry could enjoy them? Here comes a note.

"Doctor,—You seem to see our trials and tribulations and all of our needs as if you too, had endured the pangs of kitchen life for years, and this one point you have just mentioned opens up the dark recesses of our kitchens to a flood of light. And we shall all see as we never saw before that relish must exist in the person as well as flavor in the food; indeed I am almost compelled to believe you were a cook before you were a doctor. I think I may speak for all, that we thank you for the suggestion of the subjective deficiencies that may serve to cut down the toothsome character of that daily food that is ours to prepare, down in those 'depths' you speak of with such striking aptness of phrase. We shall all hope you will give us some light as to how our eaters are to be hungry enough to furnish their due share of relish at each meal."

Signed, "One of the Deeply Interested."

I am not only much pleased with this note and with the pertinence of the suggestion, but I shall also be pleased to duly consider it in the talk of the morrow.

LECTURE VII.

THE ABOLISHED BREAKFAST AND THE IMMEDIATE GAINS—A CLEAR HEAD, A CHEERFUL MIND, AND A STRONGER BODY—ABOUT MONDAY FORENOON'S WORK—AN IMPORTANT QUESTION WITH AN ILLUSTRATED ANSWER—HEAVY FARM-WORK DURING FORENOON FASTS—EMPTY STOMACH AND HIGH MARKS IN THE SCHOOL-ROOM—BED-TIME, NIGHT-HUNGER, SHALL IT BE INDULGED?—SHALL THE STOMACH ALSO REST DURING SLEEP?—WAITING FOR HUNGER WITH AN ILLUSTRATION—FASTING THE ONLY REAL APPETIZER—"WHY IS MONDAY A BLUE DAY?"

My Friends the Women:

Having abolished the breakfast for reasons that no one will care to gainsay, and with a relished dinner always a certainty, you will see an immense gain in your human affairs even in the time saved. But there is another and very striking gain to be immediately expected, a gain in physical energy for all of the forenoon's labor.

A question. "Is it possible. Doctor, that the Monday forenoon washings are going to be done with empty stomachs?" Certainly and the harder they are, the more the need will be that those stomachs shall be kept empty until nature calls for a filling. Nowhere I have a case in point. A farmer, who had been tortured for years with indigestion began one year ago to do without his breakfasts, and he declares most emphatically that his forenoons have been far the best for his work ever since. Not getting free from his stomach trouble, he came to me just before the recent harvest season for advice, when I found that his second meal was too heavy and too near his bed-time. This rectified, health and power came, and he has been able ever since to do the very hardest work a farmer ever does, until the noon-meal and with an ease that does not lose its surprise with him.

Well then, you are to keep out of those kitchens, until it is time to get ready to deal with several cases of natural hunger. And with what zest of soul, clearness of mind and energy of body you will go about it, and all the more because the work of your hands and the thought of your mind are to be appreciated as never before! For a time you will feel that you must get up very elaborate dinners, as a sort of compensation for what has not been had in the morning, but as time goes on you will find that your eaters will be more and more satisfied with those plainer foods that are far better worth the digestive energy, and hence the circle of side-dishes will get smaller. This will also be a great gain for you and also for all who eat at your table as well.

For a time your second meals will be larger than will be the need, because it will take time to dislodge the idea that three daily meals are an actual need, and that hence the two should need to equal the three in actual pounds and ounces. Of the hundreds and thousands who have actually abolished the morning meal, not one ever thought that instead of an actual cut on the average from what was eaten on the three-meal method, there is an actual raise of the average, and this becomes very significant when it is considered that what is eaten is much more thoroughly digested. Do you ask how this can be? The question is easily answered: There is so much less ailing, that far fewer meals are missed than on the three-meal régime.

Now as to the second meal, which may be considered half a meal, you will find that the need of it will so decline that it may be one of the very simplest in due course of time. It should always be so light that the stomach will be able to clear it out in time for a night of rest. And here I will give you a most assuring statement to aid you when you wish to be absent at the time of the second meal, or you do not happen to feel in just the physical and mental mood for spending much time in your gloomy kitchens, a statement you may accept as a fact, that whenever the second meal is entirely missed, the following day will be one of unusual energy and cheer. Do you not see then, in this, that when you feel that the tax upon you will be unusually heavy in the preparation of the second meal there will be the advantage of *knowing* that no evil can come, in the starving sense, if it is entirely omitted? Hunger is from habit a good deal a matter of periods. The attacks always come, whether of real hunger or of morbid want, at the usual time and it will entirely pass away and as certainly without as with the usual meal. Hence there may well be a seeming need for something at the second eating, and whether very light or none at all, nature will not take up the quarrel the same evening after the usual time of eating has passed.

I see more or less of wonder expressed in all your faces, and it is because you have not remembered that all this can be true, because the brain can so easily care for itself when there is shortage in the region of the stomach, as to not miss in the least the meals or a meal of the day; and you must remember, the brain draws its support most largely from the fatty tissues, and can do this without any apparent loss of strength, at least for a day. Now for an illustration in point.

While at the World's Fair at Chicago I had occasion to advise two young misses as to how they should take their meals while at the high school—the distance being such as to prevent having the noon-meal at home. As they could get away. from their school-work so as to reach home at 2 P. M. every day, I advised that the very smallest kind of a lunch, a mere swallow or two be taken at noon and then have the general meal as soon as they reached home. The plan was adopted, but the noon-lunch was soon given up. Now what was the result? Just this; the highest marks ever reached in recitations, an actual gain in weight of several pounds, a dinner that was relished as a gift from the gods, and no evening meal! What did all this mean for the mother? More hours of leisure, and far better health than since the prime years of the earliest maturity.

What has it meant for the mother of six children whom I mentioned. Let me tell you what that woman is actually doing every day for a family of eight children, and a boy-boarder. She is doing all the work except simply washing the ***white clothes!*** You see there is only the work of clearing away a few dishes in the morning, only a plain dinner because none other is wanted, and an evening meal so light as to seemingly scarcely pay for the getting, and such ***health*** as to scarcely ever need the family physician.

Now as to the question that was asked at the last lecture, the question as to whether we shall eat after the morning fast if not really hungry. The answer must be with an emphatic *No.* A very light attack of hunger is soon over if refused, and then if there still is not a real urgent call for food at the next regular meal, then postpone still longer; the appetite will come with due force in all cases where death is not inevitable, and with a general accumulation of powers, not only for digesting but of enjoying as well; and what is very important for you to know, beyond all question, while it is coming there is going to be no decline in power to do the work of your hands or of the thinking of your brain, nor of the functions of your soul. But here comes a very important as well as a very interesting question.

"Doctor,—You looked very earnest when you spoke of the need of letting the stomach rest during sleep. Is this in accord with physiology? The reason I ask is that I often hear people say that they cannot get to sleep if they go to bed hungry, and some assert that if they wake up at night with a feeling of hunger they are compelled to get up and eat something before they can get to sleep. What is your explanation of this?"

Signed, "One of the Converted."

I will answer this question with a *"thus saith the Lord"* emphasis. They who live on one or two relished meals daily, never, never have any bed-time or mid-night hunger. Those who do have it are sick and are travelling along that broad way with no increase of pleasure because thronged with travellers in the same direction, that *broad* highway that leadeth to premature decline of all the powers of being, and *death* before the allotted time.

You may put this down as a physiological fact which you will find no hint of in any authorized text-book on medical practice, that if the stomach be permitted to rest during all the hours of sleep, not only will the sleep be more restful but it will gain the same increase of functional power as will the brain of muscular strength. Theoretically this ought to be so, practically it is easily proven to be so.

Another question, "Doctor,—I feel as if I would like a little more light on this waiting for hunger you speak about with such energy of expression and force of language."

Signed, "Another of the Converted."

I will gladly do this. Only recently I met a gifted lady, the mother of a small family, for years she had eaten or tried to eat the usual three daily meals and in her case without any appetite. And she had never found any appetizer in the form of medicines from any of the schools of medicine. Hearing about a book called the "True Science of Living" she procured a copy and soon possessed its contents as well. At once she began a fast, and she had all the courage to endure it; she waited patiently and with large faith for four days when she was compelled to give in because she became the victim of an attack of such hunger as she had not known for years. And how her painfully apprehensive friends were confounded over the fact that she seemed to be and was actually gaining strength every hour, so that even on the fourth day she was able to ride her wheel with more energy of muscle and of spirit than on the first day.

Now I would have you all understand that hunger can never be a matter of drugs. The so-called tonics and all other so-called appetizers are frauds and are utterly void, as they ought to be, of any but harmful effects. I cannot insist with too much emphasis nor too often, that fasting is the only means that ever was, ever will be, or ever need be, to cause hunger, and to cause with it all the conditions of easy, powerful and pleasurable digestion. That you can always fast until hunger comes, no matter how long, if you are not foredoomed, not only with the most perfect safety, but also with a gain all along the line of the powers of being. In confirmation of this every case of sickness that recovers is evidence beyond question.

Have you not always noticed how much stronger every sick person becomes when the appetite for the substantials came, and do you not recall that during the restoring period, while the lost weight was being replaced what a child-like cheer of mind there always was, while the child-like powers of digestion were busy closing accounts?

You now see as you never even dreamed of before how utterly needless drugs must be for stomach purposes, and you will wonder more and more that the masters of the medical profession are sending overworked stomachs across the seas, up into mountains and along ocean-shores in a hopeless hunt for appetite, and ever enjoining vacations for the *body,* and the *mind* and *never, never for the* stomach!!! And only think of it the organ of all organs that most needs those vacations, and these are accessible to all!

These bodies of ours have been shaped by Divine hands, and while profane hands can do nothing to reconstruct them they can do everything to cause destruction.

A question.

"Doctor,—It has just now occurred to me to ask if there is any explanation of Monday being called 'a blue day' which it does in fact seem to be in all communities where the Sabbath is a day of rest from the ordinary toils of the week."

Signed, "Still another of the Converted."

Monday is certainly the bluest of all blue days of the week, and the reason why it is so, is as clear as an object in sunlight; but I will now let you go home to think of the possible solution, to take even better care of yourselves than you have done before, that you may appear before me on the morrow with keener intellects and larger hopes of the budding possibilities of your years to come.

LECTURE VIII.

BLUE MONDAY—A LAY SERMON ON THE SABBATH AS A DAY OF REST—A NEW LIGHT REVEALED IN THE TEXT NOT HITHERTO CLEARLY SEEN—SUNDAY GLUTTONY AND OVERWORKED STOMACHS—SUNDAY

GLUTTONY AND MONDAY INDIGESTION—CHURCH WORK IN EXCESS AND THE SIN THEREOF—EMPTY STOMACHS IN THE PULPIT;—EMPTY STOMACHS IN THE PEW;—CLEAR GIVING FORTH;—CLEAR RECEIVING— PREACHING WITH RECREATIVE INTEREST-LISTENING WITH RECREATIVE INTEREST;—BOTH ALIKE RESTFUL—A MINISTERIAL EXAMPLE—KEEP- ING THE SABBATH HOLY A REST FOR KITCHEN HANDS AND BRAINS— "REMEMBER THE SABBATH DAY TO KEEP IT HOLY."

My Friends the Women:

The question raised at the close of my last morning talk seems to require a short sermon to answer it as it maybe answered or rather considered. That Monday is a blue day is a matter of *fact* and not of *fiction,* when Sunday has been a day of absence of the ordinary business activities of the week, and with many a day of restlessness rather than of refreshing rest, else why should it be followed by a day of unsatisfactory feeling, doing, and thinking.

You will find my text in Exodus xx. 8, 9, 10, 11 verses, as follows; "Remember the sabbath day, to keep it holy. Six days shalt thou labor, and do all thy work: but the seventh day is the sabbath of the Lord thy God: in it thou shalt not do any work, thou, nor thy son, nor thy daughter, thy manservant, nor thy maidservant, nor thy cattle, nor thy stranger that is within thy gates. For in six days the Lord made heav- en and earth, the sea, and all that in them is, and rested the seventh day: wherefore the Lord blessed the seventh day, and hallowed it."

The central idea contained in these several texts or verses is rest, *rest, Rest* and rest because there has been six days of hard labor to make one day of rest absolutely needful. There is a sense in which this rest is to be understood that even the most learned of Biblical exegetes have failed to discover the slightest hint of, and that is that it means a rest of the whole man and not a part of him.

Now it is a physiological fact that the sudden cutting down of all business ac- tivities cuts down proportionately the need of food, and yet they are exceedingly few who do not eat far more in proportion to exercise every sabbath of their lives than they do on any other day of the week, and what is the result? A day of intellectual, moral and physical stupor, because by the absence of digestive conditions, the stomach has to labor heavily to rid itself of a mass it can by no means fully digest, hence a stupefying tax on vital power that reaches over into Monday with prostrating effect.

My attention was forcibly called to this matter recently by the experience of a sturdy farmer who, after finding that two daily meals were all that he needed for his six days of labor, concluded that one meal on the Sabbath was enough for him, and with the habitual result that his blue Monday became the brightest and the best for hard work of any of all the days of the week.

The sable lines that generally tinge the life-forces of Monday are due to the dark drapery in the stomach, a sign of mourning arising from Sunday gluttony.

You are to remember the Sabbath day to keep it holy, but who can keep it holy, serene, joyous; who can have serene thoughts, emotions of a tender or a kindly nature, for God and for all mankind, if there be relentless war in the stomach? It is the divine idea that the whole man shall rest and not a part of him, hence the Sabbath was also made for the stomachs of man, as being always the most tired out part of him at the end of his six days of toil. In confirmation of this let me inform you that ministers who have read the "New Gospel of Health" and have tried the experiment of going into their Sunday pulpits with empty stomachs, have found their Mondays days of blissful rest, tinged only with roseate hues. If there must be days of gluttony, Monday, regardless of washtub considerations, ought by all odds to be the day set apart for such heathen oblations, because the walls of the stomach, by reason of a Sunday of rest, can be better prepared for an encounter with the powers of darkness.

That minister who has never seen the light that radiates these Sinai commands, and who habitually goes into his pulpit with his head loaded with a sermon and his stomach with an assorted food mass in a state of decomposition has less love for

God on Monday, and his home will be happier if *he* gets away from it; and more, he has ever in prospect a calling to account for his premature arrival at the golden gate, and if he gets admitted, it will be as with other heathen through the remission of the sin of ignorance.

My Womanly Friends, I see your faces aglow as if astir with a new and cheering idea. And I can surmise it is due to the possibility that has suddenly loomed up before you that another cut can be made in those hours of labor, and with labor that does not harmonize with the Law of God revealed in the text. You clearly see now that the time you spend over Sunday dinners and Sunday lunches is war against *Sinai's thundering commands,* and your Sunday feeders are all going to find it out. (A clapping of hands.)

A question.—"May I ask what about the many services every Sabbath we church-workers, have to attend, as in harmony with the divine idea of keeping the Sabbath holy by way of rest?"

Signed, "One who is getting Illumined."

In answer to this I can say, that I have often been called upon to advise church workers and I have been compelled to preach to them higher morals than they have ever heard from their pulpits. I have had to say, "There is no salvation for you, nothing that can arrest your progress along the broad, the suicidal way, but that you relieve your Sundays of all excess of fatigue, in other words, attend only so far as the services are purely recreative by way of the needed change from the hard lines of week-day living: beyond this is Bin with its soul-harrowing, life-shortening results."

But how about our ministers whose Sundays would seem to be the most laborious days of the entire seven? "Six days shalt thou labor" was for, and is for, ministerial ears all the same. That minister who enters his morning pulpit as one of "the called of God," whose sermon has been thought out during hours when the brain was unimpeded by decomposing rubbish in his stomach, that man will be surcharged with physical, mental and moral energy, and the delivery of his message will be **restful recreation.** In no other than by such righteous week-day living and doing, can he be prepared to even remember the Sabbath day, much less to keep it holy and to enjoy that rest enjoined upon all. No, in the light in which I understand the echoes of Sinai's commands the Sabbath is to be a rest for the whole man, for the whole woman and for all their children. And for the best results of Sabbath services there must be resting stomachs in the pews as well as in the pulpits.

Well may your souls be roused with fresh life, for you see hope in the Sabbath as you never saw before; and your future Sundays will be such as to make your Mondays the cheeriest of all the days of the week because body, soul and spirit have become surcharged with power. Can any deny that this is the hidden meaning of the text, can any want to deny? Not those who have read the "New Gospel of Health" and have found a better way of living, because physiologically in accord with the divine idea. These would all say amen to this unfolding of the text. And you who have been sinning your lives away amid the smoke, steam and vapors of your gloomy kitchens, on the one blessed, hallowed day of the week, you will sin no more. What, rest on the Sabbath day with your stomachs turned into laboratories of chemical decomposition, keep it holy with unholy strife going on under the very foundations of the soul?

No, you will hence look forward to your Sabbaths as days of holy hallowed rest; to your Mondays as the brightest of all the days, in that you can rejoice in your strength as the horse when he paweth in the valley.

You will regard the Sabbath as evermore a day of rest in that deeper sense, as unfolded from the text. And since you behold your minister go through all his services with such a sense of joyous ease, holding forth words of life with such unwonted power and clearness without Sabbath-cooking, so will you believe can you and all yours. And all your household was often asked for the secret of the wonderful change. Now this man, in the ripest maturity of his manhood, believes the tide of time has been so turned back that he has reached the mental and physical capacities of twenty years ago; and he so rejoices every hour of the day over the great salvation that has fallen upon him, that the ministry of his time to come will be largely given to the unfolding of this higher method in daily living. He realizes as never before that there must be physical behind moral culture; that there must be physical health where there is moral health, and that there must be both attain the highest intellectuality.

The evidence of scores of ministers who have thoroughly tested the matter of preaching with the stomachs at rest is all one way. There is decided gain in intellectual and moral output, and if this be true of the pulpit, there will be, must be for the same reason, a corresponding gain in the receptive powers of the *pew.* In all of your holy Sabbath days to come you will breathe very much more of the pure air of heaven, and very much less of the fumes and vapors of the kitchen.

I now close my sermon and send you home with your souls awake to the immense possibilities that are involved in Sabbath-keeping that shall be more in harmony with the divine idea.

LECTURE IX.

REDUCTION OF THE HOURS OF LABOR GOING ON:—FURTHER CONSIDERATION OF MORNING HUNGER CALLED OUT BY A NOTE ASKING ADVICE—"THE DYING PANGS OF A BAD HABIT"—NATURE EXACTING—SHE WILL HAVE HER RIGHTS TO THE LAST FARTHING—LABOR IN A DOUBLE SENSE CONSIDERED,—BETTER HEALTH AND ITS EFFECTS ON THE MIND: THE SOUL, THE SPECIAL SENSES, THE MEMORY AND THE JUDGMENT—A STRIKING CASE RELATED.

My Friends the Women:

We have now reached the point where you all clearly see that the average work of your kitchens can be reduced fully one-half, and all the more clearly since you see how your Sabbath work can be reduced. We are now to see how the hours of your labor can be still more reduced. But before this further and very important consideration I will read a note I find on my desk.

"Doctor,—When you suggested that we should appear before you with resting stomachs I felt that I should not be able to appear, but I made the effort, and though with much weakness and apprehension, I succeeded in appearing, and soon after the morning talk began I forgot my fasting condition, and when I started on my homeward way I was surprised to find the morning lassitude all gone. And every morning since I find I am gaining in every way. Now I could but advise my nearest friend, who has long been a debilitated sufferer, and she too was induced to try a morning fast, but I am sorry to say that it does not seem to work well with her. She says that not only does she get very faint before her belated meal, but she has attacks of headaches as well, and therefore the scheme she thinks will not do at all for her. Now what am I going to say to this suffering friend?"

Signed, "One of the Saved."

Tell that suffering friend of yours with a "thus saith the Lord" emphasis that in exact proportion to the severity of her fasting symptoms so is her need to persevere, and for the reason that they all mean disease in course of development. Rev. Dr. Geo. F. Pentecost in his introduction to the "True Science of Living" has called them, with striking force "The dying pangs of a bad habit." They mean far more than the pangs of a habit, they are veritable signals of death that should rouse the victim to the most persevering efforts. You will find that she has already exhausted all remedies and means, and that her life is drifting along in a gloomy enduring sort of a way, and this has gone on so long, that time will be required to reverse the forces of life. Tell her that while she is listening to, and enduring these plaintive, peevish, even spiteful voices of nature crucified, the resting stomach will go right on regardless of all moans or complaints, and rest into such functional power for saving life as will be a revelation to its proprietor *later on.* With so many years of sinning how could it be otherwise?

Nature is exacting, revengeful even; she will not "lump accounts" nor strike a balance until the last item in the bill has been settled. Let her persevere if she would escape death in the martyr's way, if her life is worth the effort.

We will now go back to a consideration of how we are to still further emancipate your lives from the slavery of excess in labor. As you came this morning with lighter because stronger steps, you were attracted by the sight of a debilitated span of horses whose prominent bones strongly indicated deficiency in the oat-bin. They were hitched to a plough, and by the stimulus of a whip and the encouraging yells of the driver and holder, they were turning the soil by fits and starts. There was in this case a division of labor, the labor of pulling and the labor of getting the pulling done. So you often find it in your own experience; you find your work labor in this double sense, the doing and the getting your tired bodies to do it. How think you, would it seem if you could meet the duties of your life with that ease that comes from strength in reserve, with that spirit and energy, that bubbling, boiling over of life's forces we see in the schoolyard during recess?

Would it not mean time saved through the larger means of doing?

In another field you saw a team walking along with even tread, as if the plough were only a weight to ensure steadiness of motion. No sharp cries rend the air, and the labor went on as if it were only a natural means to expend surplus energy—there was strength accumulated and kept in reserve because there never was a deficiency in the oat-bin.

Working on surplus strength do you say? Well, does this strike you as a new idea, fitter for the "baseless fabric of a vision" than for sober contemplation? And yet already you have begun to have hints of a new power within you; already you have begun to go about your duties with more spirit, with more lightness of soul. Somehow the sun seems to shine a little brighter than it did, and you go about your labors with less of the driving, goading need. Somehow you find you are making fewer mistakes, hence are not laving to do over again as you did. You seem to see more clearly than before, how everything should be done, and your daily tasks do not seem quite so long or so large. And you are not so speechless any more; indeed your soul seems to be accumulating reserves, and hence you talk more and more cheerily; and you also find that those prattling children by their ways that do not tend to good order, go about with less danger of withdrawing an electric charge of red-hot emotions.

As there is more sunshine in your souls, so it shines upon all about you and other souls are made to shine. Said one woman to me, "I have no language with which to describe the change that has come over my husband's temper since he began to live this higher Christianity. Had you lived with him before and since, you could know something as I do." What will it not be to you if you can get so strong that your household duties shall become recreative exercise? Only think, even your sense of vision would become more acute and your hearing, and every mental faculty would become instinct with power, so that you can plan all your affairs more wisely, even your memories will become stronger, hence not only will you enjoy your reading more keenly but you will forget less the little matters that hinder business progress. Is all this ideal? Far from it. Every hour since you began to live more nearly in accord with this divine plan in body, soul and spirit you have been undergoing regeneration, and it has been an adding of fresh life to every molecule of the body and to every possible moral instinct and power of mind.

One of you has told me that she can even thread her needle now with the naked eye and read when it was formerly wholly impossible. Does this not mean keener vision for all the beauties of nature and a brightening of the mind, the soul's eye? Oh! the power of a genial soul alive with the strength of health, to lighten and brighten other souls, and to send its rays into the dark recesses where human life has to exist, no matter how lowly the estate, how barren the means!

My hard-worked friends, how do you think it would seem to go about with something of your school-day exuberance of strength, anticipation and cheer? And how would it seem if the heavy days of toil could be met with something of the "pawing in the valley" reserves, as if you needed something taxing to relieve the excess of energy that is fairly "spoiling" you for a "fight" with a severe task? In such a condition labor becomes a recreation, with all who find pleasure in having anything important to be done with due energy and efficiency.

And is it possible, do you ask, for you to reach anything of this school-day energy and cheer? Very possible to get nearly to that physical well-being, and therefore the mental if you can but get into completer harmony with the restorative powers of being. You are now on the highway to a higher life. You have already found that you can be about your affairs several hours before you feel the least need of food. This is a great step in advance; and not only this, you have found a degree of mental clearness during all your morning hours you never experienced before, hence your work goes on with a stately sort of grace just as those round-bodied, well-fed, shiny horses take the plough along as if it were only a check to hold down to a steadier, slower movement. Your work has gone on with cheerful ease because vital power has not been diverted to deal with unbidden food. All this you have seen, have felt. You, by virtue of well-balanced minds, will see in advance the folly of trying to do more than one-half of your daily labor in the first half of the day; in other words you will try to avoid a reaching ahead into the work of Tuesday and mixing it with the work of Monday, for you will be quick to find out that sufficient to the day is the labor thereof, and that excess of fatigue will be visited upon your stomachs, and hence starvation will begin, and that a starved body means an impoverished soul.

You will soon become aware that your brain keeps the books and that all sins against the law of being are kept in its charge. It is the delicate life-gauge of the body showing instantly as the most delicate thermometer, how the machinery is being affected by excesses. You will always so guage your daily tasks as to avoid excess of fatigue at your daily meals and at your bedtimes. To make you see very clearly the point I would get at, I will give you an illustration from real life.

Mrs. P. a farmer's wife, weight 220, who does all the housework for the family of three, and all the city marketing, with headaches her abiding enemy, and always under the need of goading the heavily handicapped muscles to their weighted tasks. Now I was able to persuade this always tired, cheerless woman to stop in midforenoon, before the exhausted stage had come, and get a simple meal which would be a rest to the body as well as a matter of nourishment, and then she could get the heavy midday meal for her ravenous, robust eaters with a great deal of zest of body and soul, taking her second meal with the family in the evening. She had the sense to take my advice and hold fast to it. And with what result? It required more than two years to get back to the twenty years before, but improvement went on with stately grace of movement, and there have been *six years* of absence of even hints of headaches, and with rare exceptions of any other ailings, while the muscles have been relieved permanently of forty-five pounds of absolutely dead weight, even as if her garments had been relieved of that weight of a padding of shot. You see she went about her morning tasks and waited until she got an appetite which always came before the powers of body were unduly fatigued. She was obedient to the divine call, and there came such regeneration that from the very first day, she not only gained in health, but found that the forenoon extra meal did not cut down the total amount of labor performed, for as health came so did ability to do more work every hour.

In the course of time, she found she could as well wait and take her first meal with the family, because the morning of labor did not so fatigue as to disable the stomach from duly performing its work, and she also found that a midday meal rendered such service as to require only the smallest of luncheons for the second and last eating.

As for the husband and the two sturdy sons, even with the long forenoons at heavy manual labor, by a slow process of evolution, had their morning's repast cut down to a degree that involved only the least time to the busy, always cheerful, strong, and healthy maker of the home.

My laboring friends, what would it have been to my purse had it been in my power to so revolutionize the health habits of an entire family with such beneficent, because permanent results, had it been wrought with a secret remedy of my own devising! No headaches, no human ailings are ever cured with drugs, for all are simply the symptoms of violated law largely and clearly avoidable. The world is yet in the densest darkness as to any clear conception how disease is caused, and how it is cured.

Headaches are always ***attacks,*** and a mysterious something to be attacked by tangible means that may be handled, seen, tasted and felt. Not for disease are simple washings in Jordan; the superstitious need is for mystic means, and whether in the hovel or in the palace.

In my next lecture we will all bend a little lower as nature is made to appear in clear perspective.

LECTURE X.

CARDINAL VIRTUES—SELF-RESTRAINT IN SOCIAL "TEMPER" IRRITATIONS—SELF-RESTRAINT IN TABLE TEMPTATIONS—WHAT TO EAT, IN THE LIGHT OF NATURE—PRACTICE VS. THEORY—BILLS OF FARE-DIET SCALES ARRANGED ON GEOGRAPHICAL LINES—DESSERTS—FRUITS—CHEMICAL AFFINITIES—DE-COMPOSED GASTRIC JUICE.

My Friends the Women:

I begin the lecture of this morning with the suggestion that there are two cardinal virtues that you will need to duly and daily consider as you work out the salvation that has not an element of pardoning grace in it. First is the virtue of repression, of a larger restraint over the results of the smaller social irritations that shoot out like electric stars, in the impatient words that cut, tear, rend. The shining face, the soft word is digestive stimulus to all within electric distances. The repressed word when the electric charge is not too great, seems to disappear by a harmless diffusion. I know this because I am very subject to a cumulative electric condition, and when well charged my conscience always bids me to a withdrawal that is not attended with a halo of sparks—and this is the better way, and especially for the nearest friends.

The other virtue is also to cultivate a self-restraint by avoiding a too violent attack upon the spread table when hunger extends her hearty invitation; hasty words and hasty eating, form a bad couplet, and in their reactive effect, soul-power is impaired. Before going further in the regular lecture I will consider a question asked by one of my auditors.

"Doctor,—You have made it very clear when and how we are to eat, but you seem to say nothing as to what we are to eat. There are so many strong views and beliefs, so much said as to what and what not to eat, that it would naturally seem that something very decided might be expected from you, who seem to believe that proper eating is the very essence of the culture and maintenance of health."

Signed, "A Strong Believer."

I am very happy to have this question come up at this most opportune time, because I have some very decided views on this subject. What you wish is to have me suggest bills of fare. This opens up a wide field for discussion, but I shall not discuss it at length. There is one law of digestion which is immutable. Natural hunger is the voice by which nature indicates what food she needs to restore her waste, and the kind she never fails to ask for is the precise kind that you will most keenly relish, and therefore bring the best results. There is a great deal of between-meal discussion as to what we shall or shall not eat, but with even the most eccentric theorists, nature generally manages to have her own way at meal-time, to the extent that there are very few who will persist for any great length of time in eating what they do not relish as a matter of theory.

Hence I do believe, I must believe, that nature will indicate unerringly what food to eat if we permit her to speak, if as I have said, digestive conditions are duly guarded. As I have said, fine theories as to what we should eat are for between-meal consideration; they go down, bend very low in fact, before their imperial master the *relishing sense,* at a well-spread table.

I will now present this subject to you in a new light. You ask for bills of fare. I could easily do some suggesting to an ailing one under the watch-care of a daily attendant, but I would have this Course of Lectures equally applicable to an audience of women of any nation or tribe in all the earth. Hence I would need to let the

South Sea Islanders eat their bread-fruit, the Chinese their rice, and the Esquimaux their blubber. You never thought that beginning at the equator the food scale gradually changes to the very utmost limit of human habitation. You easily see that I cannot very well advise that the denizen of the equator shall have blubber added to his bill of fare, nor that the Esquimaux shall have oranges and bananas added to theirs, indeed I cannot see how I am to avoid letting the people of each tribe and nation rely on the natural and therefore the available food to be found on their own lines of longitude.

We of the temperate zones, where we have the greatest mental and muscular development, require a mixed diet; in the regions of eternal snow and ice, where the only need is enough of brain to furnish motive power to the machinery, and enough of mind to capture game, fuel-food is nearly all that nature asks for or can use. An no matter on what line of longitude, *gluttony can exist,* and it does *shorten life*.

Nature can and does make her own bill of fare for all peoples, no matter where they exist. With the power to indicate *when* and *what,* with brains to indicate *how* and *how much,* there would seem to be very little need of trying to have bills of fare laid out on lines evolved in the laboratories of the analytical chemist. It is useless to theorize on this matter, for the masses of every nation on earth are compelled to live on the foods native to each, and they must so continue to live if they would live at all.

Your brain-worker may sit beside the muscle-worker and his limitations will be starvation to the other. Your muscle-worker can sit down and with relish convert ham into muscle energy, while your brain-worker can convert that same food into a *mass* whose foundations should be laid with that hilarious drug ipecacuana, or other disgorger.

The table hour is always a balancing of accounts, in which each must settle for self as the deficiency indicates, and he must do it for bills of nature's own presenting, or there will be stringency in the markets. On the question of what we may eat, nature's voice may be duly heeded if it can be duly heard. I can assure you that your experience will be, that as time goes on you will find your taste becomes so natural that you will hardly ever want any kind of food that you cannot eat with impunity, if you eat with due regard to the chemistry of digestion, for you know that you are to study to have your food-hour the cheeriest of all, and you must ever eat so slowly, so thoroughly, as to reduce the possibility of a surplus to a minimum.

"But Doctor, what about fruits that are so generally believed to be healthy, or **wholesome,** as you would have it?" This is a vitally important question, because there is not one person in a hundred but would be surprised to learn that the luscious-looking, luscious-tasting pear, apple, peach, or any other kind of fruit whatever, is without any question **between-meal gluttony,** and for the reason that they have to be handled by the stomach before it is done with a task that very generally exceeds its between-time meal hours to effectively perform, and hence the disease inciting tax of decomposition. I never sit at my own table without one eye of observation duly open, as to whether the wife and the three sons are duly enjoying those plainer foods that are well worth the chemistry of digestion. And I can assure you that there are no boys in all the city who can go by fruit-stalls with a more indifferent air, with so little of Adam's weakness.

Now I must tell you that the use of fruit in these later times has raised a nice and most interesting point in the affinities of chemical combination. According to Sir Wm. Roberts, M. D., F. R. S., (who is the highest authority I know anything of as to the chemistry of digestion), fruit juices or fruits contain salts of potash in combination with a weak vegetable acid; hence your luscious apple, that looks so innocent and is so very tempting, and which is believed wholesome to take into the stomach at any time, and always without regard to already distended stomach-walls, this apple I repeat, as soon as it reaches the stomach has its potash brought into the presence of the muriatic acid, which exists in a free state and as one of the constituents of the gastric juice, and having a stronger affinity for the potash salt than the vegetable acid, seizes upon it and at once potassium chloride is formed, and the result is a sour stomach from the irritative feebler acid. Fruits then, weaken the gastric juice by decomposing it, and hence only those who can rapidly generate it can eat apples, pears, peaches, etc., with safety. If they are to be used at all by those whose stomachs are weak, I should say with all emphasis never until one substantial meal every day has been duly digested, and let them be indulged as a second meal. They contain so little nourishment as to scarcely pay for the expenditure of stomach chemistry.

After the many years of observing at my own table, and knowing the power there is in the thorough digestion of substantial food to prevent morbid between-meal hankerings, I can say with all emphasis that I prefer that my sons allow other sons do all the fruit-eating, if fruit must be eaten as between meal luxuries.

The chemical facts I have given you cannot be gainsaid, nor can it be denied that as fruit is generally eaten, it is a surplus tax on stomach-power, a tax always in excess of the natural tax-limit, and they who are the greatest gluttons have the least of that between-meal felicity of human comfort, that Eden luxury of life that *was,* before the tempting apple-tree discovery.

You quizzing folks have turned the lecture of this morning into a talk, *ad interim,* hence I shall be compelled to dismiss you with these new ideas to take up the postponed subject on the morrow.

LECTURE XI.

EVOLUTION OF DISEASE—EVOLUTION IN CURE-DOSAGE—BROKEN BONES AND WOUNDS, AND HOW CURED—A COMPREHENSIVE QUESTION—CHARACTER OF THE AUTHOR'S SERVICES IN THE SICK-ROOM-TWO ADVANTAGES HIS OWN, AS IF SECURED BY A PATENT RIGHT—AN IMPORTANT CASE OF MISSION WORK—A CONCLUSIVE LECTURE.

My Friends the Women:

I am to talk to you this morning with a view of a clearer insight as to nature's power in disease. You have already been informed that the first step in every disease is the first failure of the stomach to meet the demands of the wastes that go ceaselessly on with every heart-beat, now most rapid as in the most violent exertion, and now least as in the calmest repose of perfect sleep.

Already you have some conception that disease is a matter of evolution, slow or rapid, as determined by hereditary conditions and the degree and persistence of the numerous causes, avoidable or otherwise, that directly depress digestive function. The more you have reflected on this question, the more clearly evident it has seemed to you that disease is never so much an attack as it is a summing-up of the results of causes that began with the birth of the individual.

Already as you have gone to your homes to those keenly-relished dinners, you have realized a sense of defensive power against attacks of disease you have never known before. And almost without any theorizing, you have lost all interest and anxiety as to germs or germicides. Here I will suggest that I may deepen your sense of the importance of a more rational conception of the origin, and therefore of the cure of disease, that you and I are not going to live long enough to see it satisfactorily demonstrated that disease has a germ origin, much less to see it cured by the convenient means of a hollow needle, through which the life-blood of broken-down old horses shall be sent as a germ-destroying spray beneath sensitive skins. While we are waiting for the golden age of medicine, when disease can be paralyzed before it begins and we can let the wind blow where it "list-eth," no matter how heavy with germs, and can exist, drink, eat and sleep with the utmost abandon, if only our needles are kept duly loaded; until we reach this age, we shall need to do the next best thing, avoid all clearly defined causes and be content to let nature do most of the curing.

The cure of any and all diseases is an evolution in reverse. He who drinks alcoholics until his stomach no longer even holds water and his mind has become the terrified victim of fantastic fears, gets well by the reverse means of the total abolition of the causative agency. He who gets in his bed with a typhoid fever must be kept free from all causative agencies until the strike is duly settled, and nature will do her part in the prevention of all hindering cause by way of the stomach through an aversion to food that should be heeded.

In this matter of disease by evolution I cannot impress you too deeply that you may clearly see the Divine hand in the cure through an evolution in reverse. To begin, know this, that *disease* in its structural changes is a matter of nature's own work, as clearly her own as in those structural changes by which the body was originally developed. This you can believe easily and without even a hint of wonder. Know this also, that the *cure of disease* is as much nature's own work in its structural changes as in those changes by which the whole body, in "human form divine," was originally developed. Now this is as clearly reasonable as in the other case, and yet you *wonder* and *wonder* and will *wonder again,* but will not be able to suggest the shade of a reason why it should not be so.

You are all so used to seeing human ailings dosed, and those doses always prescribed with such a depth of meaning and with such wisdom and gravity of manner, that you have attached to them an importance infinitely beyond their deserving, and your capacity for wonder will reach the utmost straining limit when I, a general practitioner, whose sole business for many years has been the care of the acutely sick, when I tell you with even severe gravity of expression that dosage is the most unsatisfactory means to an end that mortal man or mortal woman ever engaged in, unsatisfactory because void of science, unsatisfactory because futile, as it can but be of curing effects generally.

What! disease not cured by doses? For some time to come I would not care to handle a severe case in any of your families because that idea is too large to be received and assimilated at once. It must first reach you with such force as to stick, then it will require time to germinate, and a good deal of time to become vitalized truth. We all have our fetishes, and those which have been under superstitious adoration for a lifetime are not to be easily dethroned.

Now if any of you should get so serious a thing as a broken bone, one might think the curing would be a difficult task; or should a member of your family have a limb amputated, say in its largest diameter, there would be a great wound to be healed. All this you see, and if I were to handle the case day after day, I could do so with delicious ease because you would know that the structural change involved in the cure could not be a matter of dosage at all, not even in the least sense. The bone has to get well without salves or liniments. The amputation wound also gets well without a suggestion of healing salves or lotions.

But, *but,* once a prostration from some acute sickness and your developing faith would not be strong enough to *trust me to trust Nature,* for do not remedies cure? Not yet are you able to see except in a dim, wandering way, that nature only, is behind all destructive, constructive cell changes involved in the cure of disease.

You are now ready for that larger question you would ask, "What are you doing, what have you been doing these many years in the city of your choice to emancipate woman from the slavery of home-making, what to brighten her life through the relief of her ailings by the science of cure, and to save from premature wreckage, mental and physical, by the science of prevention?" The answer to this comprehensive question involves also something of an unfolding of a higher method in professional service. Very naturally you may ask, "What can your services be worth as a physician if you do not dose in the sense of the supposed need?"

On this subject I am able to speak with a wealth of illustration that would extend this course of lectures far beyond the proposed limit and yet not the half would be told. At this point I may very properly suggest, that with the great majority of my fellow-citizens the fact that the brain attends to its own feeding during sickness, and that the cure of disease is a matter of nature's own handiwork and not a matter of drugs is wholly unknown, and hence the idea that my services to the sick are a positive danger to life in that I fail to duly attack disease with remedies and keep up the strength with feeding, whether or no the stomach objects, is always a matter of good, honest, unselfish apprehension by sympathetic friends. Now for an illustration fresh from a recent experience and in the case of the woman already referred to as having for seven years had her forenoons begin soon after four o'clock.

I found a case of severe bowel trouble which for a few days required pain-relieving doses. Now I did not need to know the cause behind the symptoms to intelligently treat this case, but that future attacks, *strikes,* be prevented I must seek the cause or my whole duty as a wise adviser would not be done, and I soon found that these seven years of long, wearying days were behind the scenes; Hence my daily visits became a series of short lectures on the need of improvement in "home rule."

I had leisure to do this, for I had two supreme advantages, as in all sick-rooms, that are as much my own as if I held them by a patent right. First, I knew that my patient would not die of starvation for at least several weeks, so I had no figuring to do as to what dainty bit might be so daintily prepared as to be coaxed into the stomach. Second, I knew that the cure would be all nature's own work, hence, being aware of this fact, I could spend more time in shedding my light generally in the family.

The first wrong to be righted was to relieve a young daughter of the early break into sleep for the sake of getting general meals ready for human lunch-pails, to relieve her from the trouble of dressing and then spending an hour over a needless meal only to go back to bed later to balance nature's books. I soon had father and son convinced of the cruelty of their ways, and also that they themselves could get easily all the breakfast they needed and with such quiet as would rouse no needy sleeper. This at once changed the arising time of the immature girl to 7:30 A. M. And hence long before my services were ended the breakfast was practically abolished, for the stalwarts soon found that since they must get their own breakfast a very small one would do, and to their surprise it seemed to last much longer than the larger one.

Now my patient had to wait for fourteen days before appetite came, but she waited patiently without any apprehension, for she realized as the symptoms declined that her strength was actually increasing, and she became more and more interested in my sanitary talks as the mental faculties brightened; and with what cheering, relieving force did the great thought come to her that never again would she need to get up any morning until sleep had done its perfect work! I think I never saw a happier mind than hers when the appetite came with its relish that recalled the days of early girlhood.

Now one of her sympathetic neighbors had a similar attack one year before, and she came in with large sympathy to urge her to take milk often that had been boiled with suet, that would both keep the strength and "grease" the irritated bowels with healing effect, but it took *her* several weeks to gain an appetite, and as we had no time to lose in that sort of feeding, we just waited two weeks, when we had all the appetite that could be easily managed.

In order to show you how large was my opportunity for mission work, and how well I used it, I will give a condensed expression of my daily talks. "Madam, this case of bowels you have been brought to a bed of suffering with, is not an attack, but a strike, that has been gathering in force ever since you began to rob your mornings of sleep.

Your appetite failed and with it your power to digest, eating without appetite at last precipitated your trouble. Now as it took years of sinning and being sinned against to bring you to this suffering condition so must you wait patiently until the wreckage is all cleared away. You must not worry about your home-affairs, they will suffer no harm if they are not done as you would have for the time.

You have well earned a vacation, and I wish you to feel that you will prolong it until you have become rested into the power of years ago. You are not only going to get well but have the tide of time rolled back more than seven years. You will have, in all human probability another seven years of restful mornings that will give you vastly more power over your daily duties than you ever had during the best day of the last seven.

Your time-consuming, strength-impairing breakfasts have been abolished. Already your husband and son have bent low before you in contrition of heart for the thoughtless wrong of seven long years of long days, of nights robbed of sleep.

Henceforth they will look upon you through a 'tenderer atmosphere' because of the wrong endured by you through their hands. Henceforth not **He** but 'we will give the beloved sleep.' You are to sleep on every morning and take your rest, and with all the more perfection of rest, because you will fully realize that the hours of labor will bring large results when rested muscle and a cheerful, hopeful brain is behind them. And as you go on during the days of this enforced vacation, gathering strength unto strength, you will look forward to some years of a brighter life than you have ever known, and backward with the strong impression that this experience was well worth all the pangs of the illness, all the cost every way considered.

With your enlightened mind, you will never have more long days, will never try to do more than the work of a day in one day, for you will never forget that excess of fatigue not only impairs digestive energy but also prevents that calm serene sleep that make your mornings resurrections into a new world, full of fresh life, cheer and vigor. And those sons and daughters, what will it not be to them in all their years, to live in larger conformity with the laws of their lives as you will train them so to live."

I left my patient a supremely happy woman with nothing to do but to guide the eager stomach in its haste to restore those tissues of the body that the brain in its great need had been compelled to draw upon, and with what luxury of living while the over-drawn account is being balanced.

My friends, do you wonder at times when I lose my patience and become filled with a bursting charge of indignation at the powers of darkness that surround my cases of sickness and compel me to defend such services as I gave this woman, services whose good effects will go on through years and never be lost?

I will now let you go to your homes with some idea of professional methods that will prevail in the years to come, when prevention becomes elevated to the dignity of a science, when the medical science of to-day will be considered a barbarism of the past.

LECTURE XII.

A QUESTION ASKED AND ANSWERED—WHEN TO FEED THE SICK—AN ILLUSTRATIVE CASE—A SEVERE CASE OF RHEUMATISM—A DIDACTIC LECTURE TO A PATIENT—WHY STRENGTH INCREASES WITH DECLINE OF SYMPTOMS.

My Friends the Women:

I find the following question for my consideration in a note which I will read.

"Doctor,—We were all very much interested in the case of which you told us in your last lecture, and we would be glad to know farther as to what you permitted her to eat, after the appetite came.

"Signed, "The Deeply Interested."

Well, about the fourteenth day there was a clean tongue, and the sense of smell had also become enlivened so that the kitchen odors began to rouse the mouth glands to overflow. On this day soft toast well buttered was the demand, and was taken with uplifting results. This in moderate quantities and once a day seemed to fully satisfy. Next a bit of broiled steak with potato well baked was called for, and day by day the bill was enlarged and varied as the need arose.

In a case that occurred a few years ago where the stomach was locked up for thirty-three days, and hunger came only on the thirty-fifth, some broiled steak of the tough kind was permitted and with relish, but with the idea that the nourishment would have to be forcibly extracted through much mastication. My patients are always duly instructed as to the need of slow, thorough mastication, and this done there need be very little of restraint as to the bill of fare.

One of you asks about beef tea. Well, beef tea contains very little nourishment and it does contain potassium salts, so nearly in a free state that they at once seize upon the free acid of the gastric juice and rob it of digestive power. I always permit its use to allay apprehension of starving, for while it does not nourish the patient, because not digested, it does satisfy the anxious friends who give it, and with the very sick not enough can be given to do serious harm.

I am now to give you another illustration, fresh from real life. This time it is a case of rheumatic fever in a mother of forty. I was not very fresh in my reading of microbe literature, and on taking charge of the much-afflicted woman I was not aware whether any able-bodied microbes had been discovered, and charged with causative powers in this nerve-and-soul-harrowing disease.

Rheumatism in its graver forms means not less than four weeks of torture. This patient, when seventeen years of age, had an attack that totally disabled her for six months, not even being able to get out of the house during this time. Preceding this second attack there were several years of wretched existence. There was never any natural hunger, and consequently most of her meals were enforced. These would heavily tax vital power because of the slowness of digestion, and vital power was habitually further taxed because the low, depressed mental condition made labor of the merest trifles. For nearly two years the periods had been occurring every two or three weeks.

Need I enlarge on what this would do with the disposition, with the lines of expression, with the ability to be the wife, the mother, in every wifely, and motherly sense; enlarge on what it would do with ability to keep all the complicated, ceaseless round of home-making duties under easy, graceful, cheerful mastery?

How did I treat this woman? Did I need a germ killer, think you? Can you not easily see that there was enough of ascertainable, avoidable cause to indicate a reasonable line of treatment without including germs, with no known germ treatment?

Twice every day she received the relieving dose as a gift from the Gods, and each gave hours of almost absolute comfort without interfering with constructive change. Did I give her special rheumatic remedies? How could I since I did not know the essential cause of rheumatism nor know any one who did know? There was enough of stomach dosing to satisfy all the needs of *in* and *en*-vironment, dosing that did not interfere with that vacation of the stomach that nature had ordered with emphasis. The days went on with a heaven of comfort compared with the torture of the former attack, and I knew while she spent the hours so soothed, nature was at work every moment creating a new woman from an old wreck. Four weeks passed with no hint of appetite but with a marked decline of symptoms and a decline in the size of the doses.

The bed-sore had slowly healed and the fetid discharge had all disappeared; the eye had become brighter, there was more of color in the face, and the expression began to indicate a new-born life to the mind and soul. The sixth week passed, and still no appetite, but there was new strength, and ability to occupy the easy chair two or three hours daily. Well may you raise your brows, because the idea is so new to you, that the brain could feed itself and for so long a time, and that there could be the increase of strength I speak of. The forty-sixth day came and with it a clean tongue, and ability to walk about the room before even the first meal, which was asked for on this day, and a want for bread and butter was nature's first hint that the stomach had become aroused for action; and this was being taken with an unction of relish that recalled the palmy days of early girlhood, there was an expression of the very loftiest human bliss beaming from lines that were ruddy with the glow of health.

My remaining visits were largely devoted to a consideration of the means by which, day by day, year by year, causes largely avoidable had been at work with ceaseless activity only to end in the "attack"; to a consideration of the means whereby such attacks would be impossible in the years to come. Said I, "You must know that hereafter, if you will be a free woman, you must be the manager and not the slave of your housekeeping duties. You have cleared your body from all the wreckage of disease and your youth has been almost regained. There must be only the least possible letting loose of ambition that will tempt you to add more than the seven days to the weeks of your wifely and motherly duties. A keen appetite must be ever the first law of your daily eating, and this will be yours if you wisely guard and guide the labor of your hands and the thought of your brain. Those general breakfasts are henceforth given up, hence a large gain by shortening the hours of your laborious days; a lengthening of those nights of such sleep as you have not known these many years."

Two and a half months have gone, and months of wondrous childlike freedom from home-strains, and months of such relish of eating as the gods might enjoy; and the scales reveal thirty-three pounds, of new woman, as instinct with life as if freshly formed by the Divine hand. Can you imagine what it is to have the care of the sick, no matter how complicated the case, with the feeling that you **know** you have no responsibility as to the cure itself, that the brain will be better fed than human hands can feed it, and if you can but be content to stand by as a guide and a guard, all the success possible will be yours? This is just one case of rheumatism, and yet all that have occurred in a general practice during eighteen years have revealed nature's power in just as striking a manner as in this case. Every case has been a text from which to draw lessons of disease developed through clearly-defined causes, lessons of admonition that the affliction be not repeated by another course of sinning, with **opened eyes**.

In the case of my rheumatic patient there has been a reorganization of her home-affairs, not only that there shall be no more rheumatism but that other sicknesses be prevented in her family; there will be no more eating without hunger, and because of the abolished breakfasts the nights of sleep will be permanently lengthened and sufficient to the day, every day, will be the work thereof; and hence more years of life may be expected, and years that will make life far better worth living than when home was in a "valley of despair." But here is a note from one of you.

"Doctor,—I have been intensely interested in the case of which you have spoken, and it seems little short of the miraculous that such a recovery should take place with such simplicity of treatment, and to my mind the actual miracle was reached when ability to walk about the room on the forty-sixth day came, and really before any food had been taken. Is there any explanation of the increase of strength as the symptoms decline that a lay mind can understand?"

Signed, "An Earnest Inquirer."

When I began to withhold food from my sick eighteen years ago this most intensely interesting inquiry came up with every case of recovery, and for many years there was no answer. Owing to my very feeble powers of imagination, evidence for belief must have something of the clearness and certainty of demonstrations of mathematics. In the long list of recoveries, each was a demonstration, as clear as anything in all nature to me, of the fact, but what was the solution! Now this is wholly new to you, yet when you recall the more serious cases you have seen you are struck with the fact not noticed at the time, that the appetite period of disease was one of decided increase of mental and physical strength.

The solution came to me from a table of the estimated losses of the various tissues of the body where there is death by starvation, which I found in one of the standard works on physiology (Yeo's).

Now, though there was no suggestion that in disease the sick did not need feeding because the brain had power to feed itself, except as disabled by disease, and from those tissues that could be easily spared, it burst upon me with the force of an absolute demonstration that here was a physiological fact of importance beyond estimate, a fact of which there had never been made any practical use since it had become known, and yet a fact of the easiest, of the largest practicality.

Now for the explanation. It is disease that prostrates vital power and not the loss of the two or three digested daily meals; hence as disease loses its grasp with its generally prostrating effect on the mind as well as on the muscles, so must there be increase of strength since the brain is being duly supported. A heavy dose of opium or chloral, as you know, will prostrate physical and mental energy for hours, even in some degree for two or three days. In such a case, you know well enough that when the brain becomes relieved from its grasp, there will be a return of almost the original strength, even before a morsel of food is taken; so must it be in all diseases that recover. The human body can often spare largely of fatty tissues with little impairment of strength, and the appetite of the brain is so reasonable, in the emergency of sickness, as to be content largely on fatty tissues which it will take without the aid of a commissary and appropriate without the aid of a cook. What a miracle of a means to an end is this, with human life involved in the issue!

Again I dismiss you to go to your homes and as you shall walk your thoughtful way I shall ask you to think whether if the home-idol were brought low with sickness, you could have the nerve to see it recover in a natural way or see it die a ***natural death.***

Think whether your hands will ever be so strong in such a time of trial that you can hold the weak hands while another enforces a dose that can have neither reason nor knowledge behind it; think whether your hands can be cruel when the heart is heavy with anguish!

I thought once, ***felt once,*** when the prattling idol of my home was stricken low with diphtheria, and when the only comfort I had for days, was that I could defend it against the barbarism of the accepted treatment of the time. Nature was kind, since the disease was made possible by the lifelong three meals, with between-meal fruits as the will listed. My son did not die and the cure was nature's own.

LECTURE XIII.

REFORM IN OLD AGE—MORNING HUNGER AGAIN—MISSION WORK—THE POWERS AND RESOURCES OF NATURE IN THE CURE OF DISEASE—NOT TOO OLD TO STOP SINNING—NATURE'S POWER REVEALED IN THE RELIEF OF EPILEPSY, AND A SEVERE LOCAL DISEASE.

My Friends the Women:

I find the following note on my desk.

"Doctor,—During a call on a family yesterday, where there was a very aged lady who has had a stomach trouble for many years, I ventured to suggest the 'No breakfast idea,' but at once, 'with one accord' all protested that age was entirely against such an experiment. What am I to say in such cases so environed?"

Signed, "One in Earnest."

You are to say just this and with your eyes and face ablaze with earnestness; *Morning hunger is avoidable disease* and the older one is, and the more debilitated, so is the necessity to stop sinning; that it is as safe in every possible way considered, as to cease the habit of stealing, swearing, or the bearing false witness against one's neighbors.

I am very glad to get such a question, not only to answer it, but also as an evidence that you are remembering your friends in need with those stronger hands, that henceforth are to be stretched out with helpfulness and with pleasure and power as never before. I may here mention that you of the gentler sex, by reason of your strong convictions, your intense sympathies, are peculiarly endowed for mission work of this kind. Your opposition to the advance of truth, as I have sorely and often found, is at times *red hot,* but once enlightened you work with tremendous energy, faith and persistence, and also with effect.

In order that you may follow me with a more enlightened interest, I will mention a pathological fact, as the doctors would call it, that will bend you still lower before nature which is imperial, majestic, marvelous in her restorative powers; which, no matter how ailing or how old the individual, is ever at work with no hours of rest by day, with none at night, to restore the normal condition, no less in any kind of an ailing or disease than in the case of broken bone or a wound. Who then, can be too old to stop sinning against the "flesh," and who can stop without having something added to his life? The very essence of the "New Gospel of Health" is obedience to the divine law of life, or salvation through works, unhindered by the disturbing hand of man, lay or professional. None then can but gain something if there is due obedience.

You will see the significance of this great fact when you think of the multitudes who believe their stomachs are worn out, ruined beyond redemption, because of disease, and yet who can get back the lost power, get new stomachs in fact, if law is obeyed. This revelation came to me with surprise beyond utterance, and yet why surprising, when we all know that even a very old and a very feeble person would be expected to have a fractured limb healed, or a very old person would stand an amputation if not seriously diseased. Why not then a very old person get a new stomach? Does not the functional activity of the gland structures, the muscular activity of the peristaltic movement, cause molecular death and therefore the need of new molecular life, by as much a new stomach, ***brand new?*** Hence also in all other parts weak or diseased.

There is not a week passes with me that I do not meet some victim from the "Valley of Despair" who is not weighed down with the idea that his is a worn out stomach never to be renewed. This is beautiful in theory, but the best part of it is, it is sound physiology. What think you of a stomach that began to complain in the later teens and from thence on during the decade ending with the sixty-second year, often, daily, meals were rejected, ejected with righteous indignation? Could such be rejuvenated, think you? There were eight years of painfully irregular steps towards the "Delectable mountains," but the seventieth birthday was reached with the most perfect sense of health ever realized, and therefore a stomach whether old in the Psalmist sense of age, in the physiological sense it became able to perform its daily tasks with no hint of its bodily location.

This theory will strike you with all the more force when I tell you that we of the profession can never know how much of disease that gives no hint of existence there may be in every case we are called to attend, and that in fatal cases it may be the determining factor. How great the conception then that all that can be done to save a human life, no matter how many ailings or weaknesses, will be done by nature, if duly guarded.

To enlighten and deepen your conceptions of what this higher life, this more righteous living, means for you all I will give you another illustration. Four years ago Mrs. F—of this city, Meadville, Pa., a nurse, age thirty-four, of good constitution, and free from all apparent disease, ruptured a blood vessel in the rectum by a sudden heavy lift. The bleeding was profuse. From thence the attacks were often repeated and there was rarely any freedom from pain or uneasiness. She bore it patiently until her health began to give way and it became necessary to habitually wear napkins to catch the annoying discharge, when she consulted her physician and the result, a course of annoying and futile local treatments ending with this assuring statement: "You will have to go to the hospital, submit to an operation, and be content to remain for six months."

Being a widow and entirely dependent upon the labor of her hands for the needs of her little family, with lack of means, of time, and a revolting operation in question, she determined first to seize upon the last "straw," and so during an attack, the worst of all, I was called. It took nearly two and a half years to pull down a rather strong constitution to a condition of nearly total disability. Now, my friends, do you not see that it would be a great thing if an ulcerated' rectum could be "set" to getting well without annoying and exceedingly disagreeable local treatments? Why, who could think of such a thing as a local disease so located getting well without treatment with the repeated irritations of bowel movements, movements always a hindering cause to recovery? Shall I give her internal remedies? She has a good appetite and apparently no trouble whatever in the digestive process, nor is there actually any ailing in other parts, or in general that invites a drug-store. What am I to do, then, for this woman in sore distress, the bread-winner of her little family?

I addressed her about as follows: "Madam, yours is not a case for the knife of a surgeon; you have only an ulcerated condition of the rectum, hence there can be no amputations. Could you have had time to allow the original wound to recover, you would have escaped those years of torture. The rest that was then demanded has been demanded since and given. No, not rest, but the time has been wrested from your needful toils, over and over again, until you have an obstinate, chronic disease as a result. Now, as you will not feel that you can spare time for the perfect rest the diseased bowel ought to have, for I strongly assure you that if the rest could be obtained recovery would be certain, since you will feel you cannot spare the time needed, then you must be content with a slow improvement, if there is ever to be any in your case. Now I am going to assure you that by doing as nearly as you can as I shall advise you to do, there will at once begin to be a slight improvement. Now to cure this disease, we must make the entire body sound, then will the diseased tissues become stronger. To aid us in this way you will at once give up your morning meal, and until you are well enough to care for your sick, you will fast until you get hungry, which will not be before noon or even later; then you shall have a relished meal as in your ordinary condition. You will eat with due slowness and thoroughness, and while you are unable to be about your ordinary duties you will find one good meal daily about all you will need. For a time you will have your attacks of bleeding, but these will gradually diminish in frequency and force, and ultimately if you are patient and persistent, you may hope for a complete recovery."

My friends, I am able to announce to you, that with only a little loss of time, due always to the aggravations of the periods and of overtaxings, there has been a ***complete recovery*** with scarcely a hint of a return, and this after but four months of time. Can you see the meaning of this "higher law" in this case, the general health improved, the disease cured, and all that can come through meeting the duties of life with ***reserve power,*** and the leisure that power may give, in all the homework? What is the reactive power upon the sick to be cared for by stronger hands and a cheerful, confident soul, with health and hope radiating from every line of expression? And what about those young daughters who can sleep because there is no more clatter of morning dishes to disturb?

A terrible local disease cured without local treatment! Let me rouse a curious interest: later on I will tell you how the cure was wrought and how your own special ailings can also be relieved without those treatments that rend the sensibilities of every true woman. This is only one of a series of rectal diseases, mainly internal piles, where the results were equally marked, and this has remained perfectly relieved for more than a year. Do you begin to see with a little clearness of outline, something of **natural science** versus superstitious offerings and sacrifices? I hope you do.

We will enter another home: here we shall find another dragged-out mother in endless labor, in the double sense I have spoken of. She is in the prime of life, yet there is a look as if the last friend had departed, leaving her to a life of woe unutterable. Several times yearly, when the tension becomes too great, she goes down in a spasm of epilepsy, and then there are days of mental and physical prostration, of total disability. This time the attack is the severest of all.

Let me place this call of ours four years back. I gave her as you remember some lectures on the **better way of living,** and though I had labored before, often, and in vain, this time she took heed and lo, the result! There have been four years of building up of an entirely new woman, as radiant as an Eve before the "fall," and the new woman has never been "down" with a spasm.

Question:—"Now Doctor, would you have us believe that a case of "epileptic fits" has been cured by this no-breakfast plan? No, I am not going to have you **believe** but simply **infer** that such has been the fact. Epilepsy, when not due to an injury, has demonstrated its power to defeat remedial efforts for cure during all history, and why not since we are entirely ignorant of the essential morbid condition? Since some of you are interested in unfortunates of this class I will mention that in the case of a young man who had been a victim of frequent attacks of epileptic spasms for years, and also of barbarous courses of special treatments, frequently taken, the better way of living was adopted one year ago, and there have been only three mild attacks since, and these were attributed to gluttonous indulgence. In the case of a young woman who had begun to suffer when a child and in mature years suffered attacks not less than monthly they have become much diminished in frequency, and during eight months of wiser table habits.

This is a disease that usually becomes developed early in life, and I see no reason to doubt that if the body as a whole can be made stronger, the abnormal structure deep down in the brain, that puts the human body at times in the most revolting condition that human eyes ever gazed upon, may not share in the improvement and by so much be relieved or cured. In this as in all other human ailings you see the need to get the physical structures back to the condition of the morning of life so far as human effort can avail. You may go to your homes with a strong belief that it is my conviction that the cure of epileptic fits is a possibility in most cases if nature can have all needed co-operation.

LECTURE XIV.

DISEASE ANATOMICALLY CONSIDERED AND PHYSIOLOGICALLY TREATED—THE VASCULAR SYSTEM—ITS CONDITION IN PARTS DIS-EASED—ORIGIN AND DEVELOPMENT OF LEUCORRHŒA—AN ILLUSTRA-TIVE CASE—THE WOMB—HOW IT BECOMES ENLARGED AND THEREFORE ABNORMALLY HEAVY—A DART AT PESSARIES—WHY IT FALLS AND HOW IT IS TO BE RAISED—STRETCHED SUSPENDING LIGAMENTS AND HOW SHORTENED—A CASE OF CHRONIC CONGESTION OF THE WOMB PHYSI-OLOGICALLY CRUCIFIED AND THE FAILURE—PHYSIOLOGICALLY TREAT-ED AND THE SUCCESS.

My Friends the Women:

We have now arrived at a most interesting stage of our morning talks. We are to consider the anatomical and physiological conditions involved in the cause and cure of disease with a special reference to your own peculiar diseases and weaknesses.

We know very little about disease; we see its tracks and traces and are made to feel its crucifying effects on tender nerves, but of its ultimate processes we neither know or need to know anything more than we do of those ultimate processes by which a whole body is developed from a single cell by a process of cell-prolification and cell-development. As a human body develops without the aid of the materia medica, so may we presume that cell-proliferation, cell-development, involved in the reconstruction of diseased tissue is a matter that cannot need remedial forces and agencies.

The vascular system of the whole body represents the whole body in complete outline. From the largest to the most minute, the blood channels by reason of the contractile fiber in their walls, may be largely dilated even as if made of rubber. The smallest of these, the capillaries, are so thickly studded, that not the finest needle can enter into the skin without wounding them. These play a very important part in the morbid processes we call disease; they are always at their smallest caliber when toned with perfect health. The first loss of nutritive balance causes a weakening of their elastic fibers hence a dilation of their blood-holding capacity; they become actively dilated through the irritation of pain; they become passively dilated, when acting against the force of gravity and blood-pressure. We may presume that all local diseases are made possible through born weakness of the vascular channels, hence we may presume that these channels, whether in the nasal passages, the throat, bronchial tubes or wherever, are larger than they otherwise would be, and hence there will be a slower circulation of blood through them.

Now as minute as the capillaries are, microscopic in size, there is yet smaller tissue in the form of fibers between them, and dilation exerts pressure on these to a degree, at times, that causes their destruction or death by a veritable strangling process, a choking to death. We have these conditions in boils and carbuncles. Knowing as you do, that the veins return the blood to the heart, you see that below the heart this process goes on against the force of gravity in part.

Now with these points definitely and clearly fixed in your minds let us "anatomically consider" a very common and a very annoying disease of your sex called leucorrhœa or vaginal catarrh. In all these cases the vascular system is a ***born weakness,*** and from the first there is the dilation of ***gravity*** pressure, and a corresponding intervascular, strangling pressure of ultimate fibers whereby nourishment is interfered with. Associated with this condition is always a low state of health, hence thinner blood. In the perfect health of a vigorous body the blood is rich in corpuscles, and food in a state of solution, hence the water is held in a mucilaginous grasp that is strong as the blood is rich. This grasping power goes up and down with digestive power.

In very poor health the vaginal vessels may become dilated into torturous channels or sacks; this condition results in an easier escape of water from the thinner blood through thin walls, which, becoming thickened by the natural secretion of the mucous membrane, constitutes the discharge in cases of leucorrhœa.

Now you must clearly understand that in all these cases there is a lax condition of the entire vascular system. What then think you, is the clearly-defined, the first indication? Certainly to tone down or tone up the size of those dilated vessels by a process that would make the blood richer and their coats thicker and therefore stronger. Would not this be likely to stop the leaking, think you? How are we to physiologically treat this condition other than to get the patient into a closer walk with the conditions of nutrition, or with the "laws of God manifest in the flesh?"

Do you begin to see that medicated irrigations cannot make richer blood, "which is the only need in such cases, and the only hope of relief? Why here we have (a) structural weaknesses due to heredity, (b) lessened digestive power, (c) watery blood, (d) disturbed and thinned blood vessels, (e) strangling pressure on the between tissues. Do these conditions invite *local treatment?* Are you going to let your daughters go to a man specialist for an examination that shocks every womanly instinct, and receive a treatment that is as void of science as it is always futile in result for good? What, medicated irrigations to usurp the functions of nature? Perhaps you can now see how an ulcerated rectum was cured and also why senseless art failed to cure.

Again:—At times because of intervascular pressure disease is incited, and there is an ulcer to deal with; then we shall find some pain, and therefore an active distension of the blood-vessels, as well as an involvement of the passive dilatation or that which is due merely to weakened vessels. This is the condition anatomically considered.

How physiologically treated? By going out two, three or four times a week to have an ulcer cauterized? Nature always covers her sores, her ulcers, with some protective material to exclude air and fluids, shall those of the genital track have their defensive coverings destroyed by medicated washes or caustics frequently applied? And will such hasten the curative process, think you? Will they relieve the several conditions behind the ulcer? How are we to put the irritating ulcer in a strong, healthy, curative condition, except we tone up the whole by raising the digestive power? There is no other way ever given to woman whereby she can be relieved.

A few years ago I had a young lady patient who came slowly down to, vaginal and womb trouble, invited and developed by a due amount of habitual overdoing. I referred her to a lady specialist, educated under the Masters. An examination was made, a treatment for a "serious condition of disease" was applied; in a few weeks I was informed that not only is there no relief but that it takes two or three days to get over the discomfort of each application.

What was to be done? She went to her country home (she had been a teacher) to engage in a light service of general housework. She gave up the morning meal and always awaited hunger for her first meal, and for six months the first meal was not often followed by a second the same day; indeed she found after a time that she could do more duty on one than when even a light second meal was added. There were six months of home service that *did require* general muscular activity, and that *did not require* any tax of the mind; and the "serious condition of things" that would only have become more dreadful by scourging treatments, became so relieved as to give no more hint of existence, and a life was saved from a premature wreckage. *Physiologically treated* you see. And this is only one of scores of such cases so treated, with equally marked results.

Again:—The womb by virtue of its dense vascular structure is peculiarly liable to trouble arising from weak nutrition. The veins become enlarged, hence it is weighted with an abnormal amount of blood, so the heavy womb exerts an abnormal tension on the correspondingly weakened ligaments and we have falling, or by a better expression, a sinking or descending womb. How are we going to get it up again and make it stay?

Pessaries? Of all human expedients, those instruments of torture for holding up heavily-laden wombs have as little of scientific adaptation of means to an end as mortal man ever conceived. A heavy womb with its stretched ligaments, and the dragging pains in the back, how is it to be made lighter, how the ligaments shorter and the normal condition and position reached and maintained? By mechanical means and ablutions? I should say not.

The very first moment when a fast is entered upon that is to end with hunger that womb will begin to lighten and those ligaments will begin to lift it to its place, and as you see, by a toning up of those vessels, so that they will not hold so much blood. Physiological treatment you see. Here is a case. Mrs. C. of Meadville, Pa., was the victim of a lowered womb with its dragging pain and a catarrhal discharge, and a condition of things that invited the scoring of a specialist that was fitfully contin-ued for three years with no relieving result. It was at last given up because of the failure, the annoyance, the time used, the expense incurred.

She was invited to a higher method in life and in the course of a year there were twenty-pounds of new woman added to the emaciated former one, and the pelvic organs restored to the normal condition. "Physiologically treated," you see. Can any deny that the womb descends except by its increased weight as a direct result of low nutrition which also affects the ligaments as well? Can any deny that it is sound physiology that this condition of things can only be reversed by raising the power of the stomach to enrich the blood?

What about those skinnings of the cavity of the womb called curetting? That condition which is presumed to invite the need of such barbarism has behind it all the conditions involved in leucorrhœa, in ulcers. Can a womb whose inner walls have been converted into a wound ever get another lining as perfect as was the original, think you? Does a scar very naturally, fully replace the skin, the mucous membrane?

The condition of the womb that invites such scorings is in character a catarrh only, modified by the peculiar structure involved. As well curette the vaginal, the nasal tract, the throat or the bronchial tubes, if that were possible.

If nature is given a fair chance in these cases, the congested membrane with its oozing discharges will become relieved, while the whole womb is growing lighter and the shortening ligaments are adding to their lifting power by the tone of health. You at once see that better digestion, richer blood, must begin at once to tone up those thinned, dilated, torturous pockets in the mucous membrane, hence a diminished leakage of the water of the blood, thicker vessel walls with more power of retention, and relief of intercapillary, disease-inciting pressure, by a toning down in size. Do you see all this clearly? What wonder-working hands are nature's when no heavier hands are laid upon them! Have I not often seen her power in just such cases? *Yea, verily.* And she is abundandy able, if she does not have to submit to ***outrage*** administered in the name of medical science.

LECTURE XV.

PAINFUL PERIODS ANATOMICALLY CONSIDERED WITH AN ILLUSTRATIVE CASE—ORDINARY MODE OF TREATMENT SHOWN TO BE UNSCIENTIFIC AND THEREFORE ALWAYS FUTILE—STRETCHED LIGAMENTS A VERY STRIKING CASE IN ILLUSTRATION OF THE WONDER-WORKING HAND OF NATURE.

My Friends the Women:—

You are all anxious to know whether there is any relief for cases of painful periods, and whether the surgical methods in vogue are warranted from an aspect of science. The neck of the womb is dense in structure and rich in blood vessels. Ordinarily the channel leading through to the neck of the womb is closed. At the period time the womb vessels are generally congested; in the neck this swelling of the vessels tends to close the channel, in some cases, as with a vise, and hence the convulsive, torturing efforts of the body of the womb to open the closed channel to relieve the accumulated discharges. What is to be done in such cases? It is commonly held that there is a fault of anatomy here and therefore not of debility.

A common means for relief is by gradual or instant forcible dilation of the opening, whereby nature is to be relieved of a very serious mistake. The mechanical conception is all right but the anatomical, the physiological is all wrong. Nature will not have it this way.

A few years ago a delicate, bloodless young lady of seventeen, came into my hands for advice. She had entered her period life with agonies supreme at each. So low was her general condition that even in the hottest weather her hands had an icy chill. There was no disease of the stomach but her appetite had always been fitful, and there had never been the slightest attention given to times of eating. For the previous six months she had been subjected to the dilating process for relief, but all in vain. No less than five physicians had proved that there was nothing in surgery or medical science for her.

What was the trouble? Why *of course,* the weakened neck vessels of the womb by dilation were holding too much blood, and by reason of the period congestion, the pressure would so close the channel as to require those convulsive efforts to open the way, efforts that were agonizing.

What was the need in this case anatomically considered? Why *of course,* to so reduce the size of those terrible vessels that they could not block the way, a condition that was due to thin, weakened walls, weakened because *starved.*

How are we to treat physiologically?

Of course there was only one way to do this. The breakfast is to be habitually postponed until all the powers involved are not only anxious to receive but are well able to handle it. This was begun right after a period hurricane, and even the first day the invited appetite came, and after four weeks of such a luxury of meals as she never knew before, she awoke one morning in utter amazement—a period had come on during the night, and without even a disturbance of her peaceful sleep! Not for the crude hand of surgery was such divine healing, a healing that was permanent.

Were I standing before you to unfold miracles of some scheme of my own you would rightfully feel like making due discount for self-interest, but not so when nature is being held up before you. One more case of this kind. Miss B——a cultured, and most interesting young lady entered upon her periods with unusual severity of symptoms and medical advice in due time was called for. After months of failure the then last resort was presented for consideration, and after months of slow approach a tortured consent was wrung from the hapless victim. The rending was duly performed under anaesthetics but without avail; then a more gentle dilation was resorted to, but all in vain; that channel was closed every period time as in a vise. One, two, three years went on with all the annoying local treatments ever devised, but with no relief.

The fifth year came with its "hope deferred", for there was a union of hearts awaiting the issue; but more hopeless now than ever because the conscience of the hapless girl forbade the union of her martyr life to a healthful one. Friend after friend urged the hopeless mother to try the new method in life, but no, there was no apparent trouble with the daughter's stomach, hence no relief could be expected from such means for such an ailment. Finally, to satisfy the anxious friends I was called as a last resort. I found the hapless, hopeless girl yet in bed the seventh day, from the worst period she ever agonized through, and a period that threw her into a frightful convulsion before the blocked way could be forced open. There had never been any trouble with the stomach, and not one of the half dozen specialists who had gone down in defeat, absolute, had ever given a hint that it was in any way involved in the case. I could only promise a decided gain in the general condition; as for the local, perhaps there was a permanent contraction of the channel as a result of the wound of dilation.

A whole month followed of a glorious revival of the general condition. A month of such hope, of such aspiration, of such interest and happiness in all her human affairs as was never before in all her period life. Again her time of trial came, and it was the most comfortable of any during the five long years. Another month of health, culture and growth, and still more relief in the times of trial. Another month of growth, and still another, and then the long deferred marriage took place. Some years have since passed, and it has been found by experience that when the body is well toned, with health, the times of trial are often only of average severity.

Not for the crude hand of surgery is such divine curing.

All this was very simple: she only had to wait every morning until she was hungry, and then she ate as dictated by the sense of relish as does the wielder of pick and shovel. And the first relished meal had its toning effect on those terrible vessels with their thin, stretched walls that had caused the years of torture. And not only these but the entire body began to tone up; the mental, the soul-change, was not less striking. Favorite studies were taken up with fresh energy and she became as one born again in all that made life of any worth.

Can you not now see with absolute clearness, that in order to keep the way clear, the vessels of the neck of the womb must be so keyed up with the tone of health that they could not give way and close the passage as with the relentless grasp of a vise? This casè had all the resources of the best surgery of the day. In more modern times the relief can be made permanent by amputating the ovaries!! And such might have been her fate had not relief come when it did. And how many women have been so unsexed, and needlessly so, is a matter of conjecture. The surgery of the female pelvic organs is rapidly becoming a matter of dextrous knives, with hapless, despairing women the shrinking victims laid upon the altars of ambitious, expert specialists. What do you think of slashing a bloody way deep into the groins on a "hooking" expedition for the round ligaments, that they may have a "reef" taken in them, so as to hold in steadier poise the top-heavy womb? How long will it be before the shortened ligaments will stretch out again? Is it "old fogeyish" to suggest that the hazards of such operations are not warranted by any promise of permanent good, anatomically, physiologically, pathologically considered?

Nature is never absurd; she never expects to do what the knife can better do, but she can shorten the round ligaments to a far more permanent effect than can human fingers, aided by a knife, if she can have all her needed facilities granted. True, it will not be so rapidly done, but life will go on with no hazards while she is at the helm. Now as the womb is actually heavier during period times because of the increased amount of blood it contains, you easily see the need to do as little standing, walking and lifting as possible that the patient ligaments do not get too exhausted from the extra tension they are subjected to and thus lax their grasps.

The history of the woes of "fallen" wombs is by a good deal a history of abuse of the holding-up power of these generally abused appendages during period time, and you now see how and why with clearer vision than before. For years, or since I began to get over my own blindness, I have laid a great deal of stress upon the need of period rest, and that the hips should be so elevated during sleep that gravity will relieve the tension of the ligaments whereby they also can have a night of rest. There is also great need to guard the stomach carefully during these times as there is always a degree of mental and nerve unrest that has its disabling effect on digestive power.

I think I have now made you see very clearly that there is no relief to be reasonably expected from the resources of mechanics for uplifting power; that in the case of abnormally weighted wombs surgical loops in the round ligaments are not going to abolish their disposition to stretch when they are habitually subjected to double stretching force. I am not well up in my reading of the recent mechanics and surgery of stretched ligaments and weighted wombs, therefore I am ignorant as to whether they are any well authenticated cases of success from the ligation of the arterial supply of the womb and ovaries, by which they would very materially lose their power to complain when abused, through an atrophy from starving.

What then are we to do in cases of fallen prostrate wombs in their worst forms? Let me give you a very large idea. You recall how the rheumatic woman became a new woman in a short time after the weeks of lying in bed; how the abnormal periods were relieved and a local trouble that may have been an ulcer, associated with a bad chronic vaginal catarrh, was also wholly relieved. Now, why cannot such means be taken for relief without a course of rheumatism or other protracted acute disease as well? It is my opinion that a course of lying prostrate with elevated hips for a month or more with the meals physiologically adjusted would prove the swiftest and most permanently effective means ever adopted for relief. Let me show you what nature can do when she has a chance in a surgical case.

Early in this year "'95" after an absence of some months, I found a lad of fifteen walking about our streets in pursuit of an appetite, he had only been out for a short time after a terrible siege with appendicites, barely escaping with his life. His stomach was being coaxed several times daily with "tonic stomach bitters", and up to date they had failed to coax. He was at once put on a fast unto hunger, and from thence the appetite became a matter of daily regularity, and for a whole month daily improvement became a matter of conspicuous notice, so much so that I did not even think to ask whether there was yet trouble in the offending groin; after a month my attention was called to the fact that there was still a hardness that was not getting better.

I soon found that in the region of the recent attack a grave surgical operation must be resorted to, to relieve a developing abscess. With a month of daily eating with keen hunger, there had come color to his face where there was none, and brightness to dull eyes. Nature had become prepared for a "tug of war." During all the days and weeks of his acute attack every one of his three daily feedings had been enforced, and each had been put into *a dry torpid stomach, dried and torpid* from the frequent doses to relieve pain.

The surgeon came and with due care worked the knife deep down to the enemy of the young life, and a bursting charge came forth. His feedings before, as you are aware, were to nourish the brain, hence to support vital power.

This time we are to let the brain do its own feeding. The shock of the grave operation, the pain following, and also the depressing after-effects of the anæsthetic very effectually took away the good appetite and, we may well presume, with it the power to digest food, and yet surgeons do not wait for a return of appetite, but rather begin to have food put into stomachs as soon as they become able to retain it.

In this case we waited until noon of the third day when there was a call for broth which satisfied all the needs of that day. The fourth day a bit of soft toast was taken with keen relish; the fifth, chopped beef with baked potatoes, and from thence one general meal daily was taken, reinforced by a very light evening lunch, and all this while lying in fixed posture on the back. The anxious mother being duly instructed that the relished meals were the strongest possible evidence of hope that the life would be saved, prepared these meals with sparkling eyes, and not with groanings of soul as before. Now when I tell you that the wound was two and a-half inches long at point of incision, that it was five inches deep, that on his back with no exercise at all, after the fifth day, the bowels acted naturally and daily, that on the fourteenth day he was dressed and spent the day in the sitting-room, from thence going to bed only at night, that on this fourteenth day there was a ruddy face and apparently an actual gain in muscle weight, that since, by adhering strictly to the two daily meals, he has acquired a degree of robust health he was an utter stranger to before, ***perhaps*** you will think there may be great possibilities for ailing women by entering upon periods of absolute rest, with meals confined to periods of absolute hunger, as the ***swiftest*** of all ***human means*** for growth into the normal condition, local and general.

Nature is a wonder-worker when she does not have to spend a great deal of her precious time and power in disposing of food that cannot be digested. This young lad never, in all his life, had such a rosy complexion, such bright eyes as were his, even before he got out of his bed. And how simple the means! He only had to lie on his back and let himself get real hungry every day and nature did the rest; and never was he so safe from complications as when an empty stomach was resting into power to handle those meals, meals that were more keenly relished than ever during all his former life.

Is not this case full of suggestion of tremendous possibilities for women enslaved with disease?

LECTURE XVI.

THE REST CURE AS ILLUSTRATED IN A CASE OF A FRACTURE OF THE THIGH—How NATURE WORKS TO RESTORE LOST BALANCES AFTER THE STRIKE IS OVER—A BEAUTIFUL THEORY AS TO THE EVOLUTION OF DISEASE AS ILLUSTRATED IN THE FEMALE PELVIC ORGANS.

My Friends the Women:

In order to impress you still more deeply as to rest cures, I will tell you of a boy of twelve whose fractured thigh came under my care. You at once see that the amount of exercise he would take, during his five or six weeks on his back, would be much less than would be at that age with unrestrained muscle and mind. This fact is not taken into account by the people and very rarely by the profession as it ought to be.

The disabled boy was at once put on a 10: 30 A.M. general meal, with only a very light meal at 6 P.M. AS for the various fruits and cakes that were often sent in by large-hearted friends, these were put to decorative use only, as there was soon such appetite as to make the plain nourishing foods fully satisfy, and so satisfy that fruit did not tempt. Now I am going to assure you all that when the lad was able to use the limb, all who knew him were struck with the ruddiness of his face and brightness of his eyes, never noticed during all the years of his fresh-air living, and as for the fractured ends, there was no hint of their exact locality when he was able to take the first step. Do you see that there is a tremendous meaning for sex disorders revealed in these experiences?

If a fractured bone can be healed by resting on the back for four or five weeks, with also an increment of general health; if a dangerous wound can heal in fourteen days, in an almost motionless position and with improved general health, why may not the same means relieve congested wombs, ovaries, *stretched, tired-out ligaments,* and the anæmia of the genital track? Why? Certainly they can.

It was my opportunity to see thousands of wounds get well during the war of the Rebellion with only the simplest and no antiseptic treatment, and where death occurred their gravity or constitutional conditions were generally, and as I believe, justly deemed the determining cause. How does it come then that those concealed, chronic wounds (ulcers) and weaknesses of your sex must need so much of crucifying, local treatment? It is one of the almost unavoidable tendencies of specialism to see all the gravity there is in abnormal conditions. What then must be the effect on the mental condition of woman to be made to feel that her intolerable ailings are causes, and not results treated as causes, and therefore with failure inevitable?

Such soul harrowing ailings, such treatments and such failures, what bondage is there not in the combination?

As I understand the condition of weak and diseased structures and the conditions of cure, to my eyes the local treatments in common use, except the mechanical and surgical, are a barbarism of to-day and in the time to come will become barbarous to all eyes.

To return to our subject: I ask you to again recall how the powers of nutrition work at the close of one of those long strikes we call typhoid fever, or rheumatism, or pneumonia. Until the diminished stores are returned, there seems to be, as I have told you, a sense of relish, a power of digestion and a freedom of soul that makes the man a happy boy, or the woman one of the happiest girls. This taken duly into account, with the surgical experiences just related, why not expect even greater results by a voluntary rest of days or weeks when need be—a rest not enforced by injury or illness?

Three years ago a married woman came under my advice, a sufferer from marked general debility, constipation and three-weeks-apart periods, and these for a long time. She was tall, slender, colorless, of a naturally somber temperament, her life had been painfully endured for years in some of the ailings. She was induced to get her first meal at 9 or 10 A. M. The husband was induced to get his own as he listed, only the wife was not to arise before she cared to get up In due time there was a girl-like appetite for the first meal; but there was so much to be done, the powers of being were so sluggish, that progress was exceedingly slow, so that if it had been a case of drugs only, I would have been excused very early in the case. But there was no getting away from the relish and the power of that first meal. There were slow gains, but not enough to resist an attack of the grippe during the first winter, nor to prevent a lighter attack during the second winter, but during the third summer the periods became fully normal and likewise the action of the bowels. And such general health as was only hers in child-life.

Now if this woman had gone to her couch for a month, or even six or seven weeks, with her meals spaced to a ravenous relish, I fully believe that the work of three years of growth would have been achieved in so short time. In many, many cases I have seen color coming to faces and brightness to eyes, where none had been seen for years, and days before any food had been called for, and such is only the local expression of the general condition! Only think, it means for those with sex ailings, toned vessels of the ovaries, of ligaments, increased lifting power; wombs that are lighter, because their dilated blood-pockets have become contracted, and genital tracks no longer suffused with catarrhal offense! Can any specialist deny that this is *sound anatomy* and *physiology,* and that the means of relief are of the divine plan? Is it confused insight that gazes within, and recognizes the *molecular change* as the basis of regeneration, where there is structural loss, or abnormal structural change? and that this change cannot be a matter of dosing?

Again let me call your attention to the notable physiological fact, that the very moment when a rest is proclaimed to the stomach until hunger shall come, is a moment of regenerative change for all with whom death is not inevitable, no matter where or how many their ailings. Is not this thought one of great inspiration to all suffering women, hopeless because ailing, hopeless because in the hands of specialists with all the resources of machinery and of the materia medica with only failures as the result? Only think that with the very first meal which shall be so much enjoyed, the ovaries that are out of the reach of everything but the extirpating knife, the womb with its annoying catarrhal discharge or its premature opening of the flood-gates for the escape of life; the long lax ligaments, the broad suspending curtains; the open mouths of the genital tracks with their outgush of abominations, that all these *begin* to become instinct with fresh life at this *first meal!* This is rather a long sentence but not so involved, perhaps, but that you can realize without effort that it is vital with meaning, with life.

Again, not only is their instant improvement of the peculiar ailings but of all other ailings as well, whether of head, lungs, liver, kidneys, or what not!!! What a panacea, what wealth would there be in it, if only a secret remedy! Let me utter a prophesy with a "thus saith the Lord" emphasis, let the words be doubly under-scored, let me draw the curtain that obscures the future and allow you to see as you now believe that in the not-distant future, the *rest cure,* the cure according to nature, will be the only curative means that will be believed to be of any avail in all sex-ailings not requiring the surgeon's knife. And it will be found the swiftest of all means, no matter how much time will be required or demanded. Let me suppose that the complete vascular system is standing before you in the perfect outline of one of your own sex. You gaze on the ailing pelvic organs and you see that the capil-laries, veins and minutest vessels are irregularly dilated. With your huge magnifier you see that in these the blood is circulating very slowly, in some it does not seem to be moving at all. Let me enclose one of your fingers with four of mine and the thumb. See, I can so press that it pains. Your Singer represents the intercapillary fiber, mine the capillaries dilated through loss of contractile force, and the force, as you also see, contending against the force of gravity.

Look again through your glass—you see that the intercapillary tissue is smaller than in parts normal; it has a pale sickly hue as if in a starving condition; it is starv-ing, for the juices of life can scarcely enter it with vitalizing power, such is the strangling pressure. As you look with absorbing interest you see an oozing of water from capillaries and veins that have become pouches or pockets; as this goes on the capillaries and intercapillary tissue slowly disappear, they seem to have become lost or changed into a thick liquid of yellowish cast, surrounded with tissue in an abnormal condition. You are gazing on an ulcer of the neck of the womb or of the vaginal tract, and this has been the outcome of the years of disease culture. Is there any object in subjecting that morbid mass to the action of dissolving caustics or is it a case of tonic or *healing applications?* Could you watch the womb day after day in an ailing one, you would see that all the blood-channels are slowly enlarging, that the circulation is becoming slower, that the womb is actually increasing in bulk! And you see also that the broad supporting ligaments are slowing elongating and are getting a pale sickly hue and the round ligament is getting longer, smaller, and is losing its glistening lively color. Do I need to add anything to this picture to convince you that these ailings are out of the reach of the materia medica?

Again I must say that my opportunities for observation of failures, after the most persistent course of authorized treatments, is all I need, even in themselves, as evidence of their futility. Said a matron of a hospital, a refined, sensible woman, educated and trained under the masters: "The specialists in the large cities have become rich through their treatments, *but they never cure their cases*"

Again let me say that science and nature are never absurd; they never presume to eschew aid that may wisely come from mechanics or surgery. Philosophysees the thing to be done in the *every* sided aspect; it sees with insight as well as eyesight, and is ever ready, able and willing to give credit to all the forces engaged as they relatively merit; it does not hesitate ever to discard obsolete machinery or method for the improved. There is no stupor, no prejudice, in the walks of philosophy, of science, or of nature.

Said a university president to a perverse professor, who would not resign because his frankness in telling what he saw in the department was averse to dogmatic belief, "We are not going to use you quite as they did Galileo." "No, but you are going to proclaim ecclesiastic proscription in a case that can only be decided by scientific evidence" I have now given you evidence for the faith that is within me, and if you do not now see as I see, if you do not believe as I believe, you will at least give me credit for intentions as lofty from a humane, from a professional standpoint, as can well actuate a frail, mortal man, who being only mortal, may not, because of the force of his convictions, always keep in perfect philosophic poise.

In a practical sense it seems to me I have now told you about all you need to know as to those ailings of your sex that do not require surgery. With your peculiar ailings so common wherever woman exists, I shall expect each of you, after the vision has become cleared by thought, by reflection, to see emancipation, not only from their withering effects upon body and soul, but also from treatments of the heavy-handed.

LECTURE XVII.

MISSING PERIODS CONSIDERED—THEIR FAILURE BELIEVED TO BE A RESULT, AND NOT A CAUSE, OF DISEASE—AN OMITTED SUBJECT CALLED UP BY A QUESTIONER—CONSTIPATION CONSIDERED IN A PHILOSOPHIC WAY.

My Friends the Women:

I find the following note on my table from one of you:

" 'Doctor—We all left for our home at the close of your last lecture with a feeling that emancipation had received a tremendous impetus to us by your later morning talks; indeed we have been so surprised at nature's power, as you reveal it; surprised that there is such hope in a class of sufferings that thus far the science of specialism has failed to give other than failures as results, that we are almost too confused to think clearly, so overpowering do the great possibilities of cultured and maintained relief seem to be. But there is one other common ailing you have failed to consider that seems to us of vital importance as well as interest. What about the missing, the checked periods, that abiding horror of motherly hearts?" Signed, "An Earnest Enquirer."

This is a very important as well as a most interesting question, and its consideration would naturally come later in my course of lectures. It is not a disease in itself nor the cause of disease. It is simply a symptom of impaired general health, a loss of power to maintain the reproductive function. This may be due to simple general debility or general disease resulting in debility of the ovaries, whereby they remain in a condition of functional torpor. In this condition they are incapable of doing harm in a causative way, hence there need be no alarm on their account. If they can be amputated without seriously impaired health, a dangerous operation being taken into account, they can certainly remain in the condition of torpor equally well without danger. When the check is sudden it is generally due to exposed feet, or other exposure, and is rarely more than of temporary persistence, and is rarely followed by dangerous involvement.

These cases, in the largest majority, occur in starving bodies, starving because of meals habitually enforced without hunger, hence the white faces, the glassy eyes, the listless minds, the languid movements, the blood "turned to water," and the mothers weighed down with an agony of apprehension. What barrels of "ironed off" muriatic acid have been piped fruitlessly over pearly teeth to meet a supposed need in these cases; what tonics, what lashings of the stomach to drive it into functional power; what means, what methods to coax, to plead, for the appetite of hunger to come! Some of you now feel like groaning in spirit as you remember, as you recall, the picture and see it revealed in the light of nature.

There is always the fear that the failure is a retention that unless expelled is certain to develop consumption or other serious disease. In all cases associated with disease it will generally be found on careful investigation that the health began to fail long before the periods were affected. Hence the natural conclusion that failure is due to torpid ovaries, too torpid to generate anything that needs expulsion. Let me repeat, the irregularities that often characterize the maturing age may be ascribed to lack of ovarian development, general debility or disease, and these alone need consideration in all cases. I have at present a case of ovarian torpor due to developing debility that I fear is the first stage of some disease largely due to heredity, and I have no power of reason to convince the anxious parents that something is not being retained that is running riot among life's forces.

A question:—"Doctor, our questions no doubt often break in on the lines of your lectures in a somewhat incongruous way, but questions will arise even as the spirit moved, and it greatly adds to the interest when they are answered or considered as they 'come up fresh from the mint.' If not too much out of the present lines let us hear something from you about that almost universal ailing, constipation."

Signed, "Several of Us."

This is a very important question because the ailment is so universal. Daily movements are supposed to be the need of every human being, and hence no classes of medicines are in more common use than for this supposed need. But they never cure, for they have the same relation to the stomach and bowels that the whip has to the over-worked or starving horse. They are not in the least sense curative.

The bowels may go for days without movement when the stomach is duly cared for without danger to health, **when** there is no apprehension involved. The bowel contents are always so disinfected, that septic poisoning from their presence may be considered impossible. I do not now recall any suggestion in medical literature that there is danger of blood or any other poisoning from retained fœcal contents. There is one thing absolutely certain, bowel remedies do not cure, and the public is as well aware of this as is the medical profession. There is another thing just as certain; bowel remedies or scourges as they should be called, do debilitate both stomach and bowels.

You are all aware of the fact that the large bowel acts as a receptacle with strong expulsive powers. As its contents are covered with a slimy coating, with disinfecting properties, they can remain indefinitely with perfect constitutional safety. Now, for a bad case of this kind, it is necessary to relieve the mind of apprehension, and then to "take no thought" but of the better care of the stomach. In very obstinate cases I find there is more trouble to secure mental relief, so ingrained is the belief that daily movements are of the supremest necessity, than to get bowel improvement. But this once secured, then, with an infusion of the richer blood that comes from the better treated stomach, through all the mucous follicles and muscle fibers of the bowels, no more to be forced by the lashings of drugs, power will come for movements that will be regular, as determined by an active or sedentary living.

It will take time to reach this normal regularity, and for a time, and especially with those who are troubled with those anal tumors we call piles, or who are disposed to anal weakness, it may be necessary to aid expulsion by warm water flushing.

There is one thing certain, there is no relief from constipation, except from a wiser use of the powers of digestion and from an absolute total abstinence from all bowel remedies. Better digestion is your true tonic for torpid follicles, for languid muscle fiber, and these must rest while being fed. And that they may rest as nature designed, the ways of the bowels should not be blocked by surplusage cast out from the stomach.

Again I must remark with emphasis, the mind duly cultured to a complete acquiescence in a let-alone policy, the bowels, the stomach kindly treated, may be left to Nature's own prompting and with the certainty that movements will become normal, whether daily or weekly. That woman who sits in a chair with busy needle ten or twelve hours daily or weekly cannot have such bowel functions as in a case where there is a broader back that bends over a washboard as many hours daily. The strongest man engaged in the very heaviest manual labor would not have more than one movement daily if his eating habits were physiologically correct; how then can the banker, the book-keeper, or other brain workers who by reason of torpid stomachs and bowels the result of too frequent meals and too little general muscle activity in the fresh air, expect regularity except under the lash of drugs? When one habitually eats only as the need is developed by exercise, the bowels will act normally habitually whether in the invalid chair or the invalid bed, but not necessarily every day.

Just once more let me repeat, the chiefest difficulty in treating constipation is to get the mind convinced of the science, the need and safety of the rest cure. The muscle fiber of the bowels and the mucous follicles must not be called upon to handle undue rubbish cast out from the stomach, and when Nature places an embargo upon food they may rest, as should the stomach, until it is raised, whether for ***days, weeks or months, and no septic*** poisoning will thereby occur.

The only cases where I would stimulate the bowels by catharsis would be in cases of sudden attacks of disease where they had become unduly loaded through gluttony. Once cleared, whether by Nature or art, then every movement should be left to Nature, and Nature will not be found wanting. With a large experience and close observation I have never seen a single case where there was a hint of trouble from the bowels after they had become relieved from the rubbish of unbidden food.

A question: "Doctor,—What of the use of food for bowel purposes, as brown bread or other foods that are supposed to regulate the bowels?" You should never in all your life sit down to your meals with the thought of what should or what should not be eaten for bowel purposes. You are to eat to satisfy hunger, and if you are to have an enjoyable time every mouthful should be keenly relished. It is very true that there are foods that, taken in due quantities, will stimulate the bowels to the needless task of disposing of indigestible food that is received from the stomach as ***cast-out rubbish.*** I need scarcely tell you that regularity acquired by such means is not healthful either locally or generally. Nature does not ever invite us to swallow a single morsel that does not keenly satisfy the sense of taste, for unless this sense is appealed to the mouth and stomach glands fail to become interested, and hence their supplies do not gush forth as at a belated picnic-dinner where the reins get unloosed.

The sense of relish has a good deal of the human in it. It loves change, and no food therefore can be habitually indulged for bowel purposes, without a weakening of the entire digestive tract, and all the more will this be the case if the meals are so near each other as to be only enjoyed in an indifferent sort of a way. You are all beginning to see that health is largely a matter of intelligent care, that health and disease may come and go a good deal as we list. Bad health is always a matter of life-long culture, and it is our misfortune that we have no easy, rapid method by which the debt against nature can be balanced. Certainly we cannot hope for the germ-killer for our numerous chronic ailings. Nor is there hope for you, in your peculiar weaknesses and diseases, that you shall have your old account balanced in any other way than an "eye for an eye, a tooth for a tooth" sense of equity.

Nature will have her own way and very often it must be over a long thorny way. Our human ailings are our human evidences of violated law (unless the germ-theory of disease is true), and as our sins have been long and grievous, so must we repent, and do work meet for repentance, and with a persistence in works that shall know no rest until the very last grain of the last sacrificed "pound of flesh" is restored. Nature is a veritable Shylock in the persistence with which she demands a settling of overdrawn accounts. "Pay me what thou owest," is a demand voiced in every headache, every sense of pain, discomfort, every fever, in every human ailing, acute or chronic! Can it be possible that all ailings come from the stomach, I am often asked? No, not directly from the stomach, but after all they are the direct results of causes that impair its power to maintain the normal balance we call health. In this sense disease is a cumulative condition of bodily sins that, borne to the limit of endurance, must needs to be settled or death will come. Will it not be vastly better for the people to believe this, than to claim that a mysterious germ is the inciting cause, which only needs the undiscovered, ever-ready antidote to perform the needed miracle that we may go on in our old ways of sin without let or hindrance?

Let me send you to your homes with this thought; that when you have had a night of rest that includes perfect rest of the stomach and arise to go about your affairs calmly, deliberately, not eating until you can sit down with real hunger, you have kept your bodies in the best possible defensive condition against disease; in fact all this while our ailings whatever and wherever, have been on the road to recovery. Continue this and all the health and strength you have lost shall be regained.

We will have an hour of questions and answers at our next.

LECTURE XVIII.

AN AUDITOR BECOMES ALARMED OVER THE LOSS IN WEIGHT, AND HER CONDITION DISCUSSED—EVOLUTION OF OBESITY—EVOLUTION OF THE "FIGHTING WEIGHT"—IS IT WISE TO EAT LITTLE AND OFTEN?—THE QUESTION CONSIDERED FROM A PHYSIOLOGICAL BASIS.

My Friends the Women:

One writes as follows:

"Doctor, I have now been on a fast for eighteen days and have begun to get a little apprehensive over the fact that my dresses are getting quite too loose. I seem to be losing weight every day, is it possible that I am not eating enough?"

Signed, "Anxious."

I will ask the listener a few questions.

"What has been your weight the last few years?"

"About 160 pounds."

"What was it about the time you entered upon married life?"

"About 125 pounds."

"Do you feel as strong since you became so heavy?"

"No."

"Now let me ask you, if, since you have become so weighted you do not tire more easily and get out of breath on the least exertion?"

"Certainly. I feel that I must go upstairs very slowly or I will become so dizzy that I need to sit down to recover from it."

"Have you been so cheerful and full of energy, could you think as easily, remember and plan and push your work as when you got around with lighter steps?"

"Certainly not."

"How is it with you now?"

"Well Doctor, I must confess that something of my old-time energy has been coming back and for a week or more, now that my attention has been called to it, I find that I have been going upstairs without any thought about the breath, in fact I have been rising suddenly from my chair and without the dizziness that I had before or since I became so weighted."

"Are you certain that you were stronger every way when you weighed only 125 pounds?"

"There cannot be a shade of doubt about it. Why I actually believe I could do more work in a day and with greater ease than I can now do in three."

"Well as you are too young to have your strength impaired by age, how is it that you have become so disabled?"

"Well, I hardly know how it is."

"You are perfectly satisfied that you have been getting stronger since you gave up your morning meal?"

"Certainly Doctor."

"What have you been losing then muscle, think you?"

"Well, it would seem not, else I could not have had the manifest increase of strength."

"Well, now, if you were actually much stronger when you only weighed 125 pounds, and as you have been gaining strength since you have been going back to this weight, are you actually suffering any loss that needs to alarm you?"

"Well Doctor, in that light certainly not."

Now I will explain this to you. Since you began to take an extra weight, you have been losing your mental and physical strength, hence, since you have had to apply more or less of force to yourself to get about your affairs, you have favored yourself more than ever, and getting tired as easily as you have has made more times of rest needful. But all these years, by virtue of a good stomach, you have eaten about the same daily average as in the days of light weight. Therefore you have accumulated a surplus of fatty tissues, associated with more or less of bloat, and by reason of your diminished exercise; your muscles have been growing smaller while your body has been growing larger. The heart has been a great sufferer from this condition, hence, when you rise suddenly it becomes so overpowered with blood that it causes the dizziness you are so annoyed with through slow beating, therefore leaving the brain with a diminished supply of blood, for the time.

Now, ever since your meals have been more in proportion to your muscular exercise your muscles have been growing larger, heavier and stronger while your body has been growing lighter. In the language of the prize-ring, you have been getting down to your "fighting weight." When I began to advise people to go without their breakfasts, there were very frequent cases of alarm on account of loss of weight, and I was entirely unable to explain as I have done in this case. I am now able to declare to all that on the very day they begin to treat the stomach with physiological care, the body will begin to **come down** to the *"fighting weight,"* the muscles will begin to go up to the "fighting weight," that it is not in the line of possibility that there can be a loss in any impaired sense, from so regulating the meals that there shall be no eating without hunger.

A few years ago a case of rheumatism with numerous associated ailings in a woman weighing 240 pounds came under my care. Burdened by disease and undue weight she had been nearly disabled from all home duties for many months. For a whole year there was a gigantic struggle on the part of Nature to balance the books, with most discouraging progress. The case seemed hopeless; but finally the symptoms all disappeared and then began a reduction of the body to its normal weight, a process that went on for several years until there was a loss of **seventy pounds!**

The fat weight went down, the muscle weight went up with a corresponding increase of mental and moral power. Now in this case the physical sins had been so grievous that it required a year of total invalidism as the first step in the cure. The diseases relieved, then, with no care about the health other than to work according to strength and to eat only nourishing food with the mouth of hunger, regeneration, evolution, went on year after year, with life a veritable heaven on earth compared with the many years of torture hopelessly endured—not, not for **drugs** and enforced food are such triumphs as these.

This is the only way there can be a cutting down of abnormal weight, with the muscle weight increasing at the same time. All losses that come by confining food to certain limitations or by the use of "anti-fat" specifics are attended by muscle loss and consequently by a loss of strength. President Garfield probably weighed 250 pounds before he received his death wound, and as nature refused all feeding he daily lost weight and strength for weeks; his reserves were all taken by the brain until only a skeleton was left, but except as affected by pain-soothers his mind was clear until the last.

Now I wish you to clearly understand that the loss of weight that occurs when natural hunger is fully satisfied every day, is normal, also understand that no person will permit a loss that would come from unsatisfied hunger. With such a loss going on in a well person, before it would become dangerous, there would be no conscience to prevent a burglarious entrance to a well-filled pantry, if there were no other resources to meet the painfully pressing needs.

Keep this ever in mind, no one will permit hunger to so develop to the pang degree except in times of famine. Keep this also in mind, where there is daily food and daily hunger no loss can occur that is not healthful. The first impression of the no-breakfast idea is to rouse utter condemnation. The mind is made up instantly; there is no thought as to whether there is sense, and therefore science as a basis. Science never advances except where there is free thought and original investigation; science waits until all the evidence is in, and then there will be a verdict from which there can be no appeal.

When you read the "True Science of Living" I wish you to carefully note the account of the search of Sir Humphry Davy after the composition of water, as an illustration of the workings of the scientific mind of the highest character. Such a mind, by reason of the clearness in its perception, of facts and their relations, would consider it a sheer waste of time to read a single page of the best *materia medica* that was ever published except for botanical or chemical purposes. Under the head of "Medical properties and uses" the assertions would seem *simply absurd.*

Read Sir Humphry Davy carefully, and you will see very clearly how utterly disqualified he was mentally to have been the bearer of remedies into the homes of the sick. His was not the science of guessing but the science of the original investigator, who weighed evidence to find its worth and was scientifically unable to bring in a verdict, until the last scintilla of evidence had been duly considered and placed in its natural relation.

But here is another question. "Doctor,—It is often advised by sanitarians that it is better to eat a little and often, than to eat as much as one would do by getting very hungry; what would you say of this idea?"

Signed, "Enquirer."

I would say at once, that the idea was conspicuous for its absence of sound physiological knowledge of nutritive processes. Now, you must clearly understand that all diet schemes ever devised are founded on the conception that the sick are as dependent on food to support vital power as are the well, and that therefore feeding must go on daily, no matter how sick. As soon as physicians become aware of the fact that vital power can far better be conserved without any feeding at all during sickness, by reason of the self-feeding power of the brain, there will result one of the mightiest revolutions that ever took place in the annals of medicine, and this fact is to become known in the near future, and it will be accepted by the true scientists in the profession; for it is a fact so clearly self-evident, that the mere statement of it is overwhelmingly conclusive.

Let me give you a very marked example of brain feeding where the meals were small and frequent, are as always the meals of the sick. Did it ever occur to you that frequently meals do not seem to succeed well in supporting the strength and in preventing the wasting of the body in time of sickness?

I recently had in my care a man of 62 who for some years slowly wasted away because of much treatment for an acquired disease of one lung. In his primest maturity he weighed 177 lbs.; his average weight during his last healthful years was 150 lbs. For several months he was under the medication of a quack specialist whose vigorous efforts fully succeeded in paralyzing digestive power. He was able to wisely direct the affairs of his manufactory until the day before his death. During the last week of his life he visited his establishment and the scales revealed a weight of 100 lbs.! Did that skeleton have a wasted brain think you?

The brain had been forced to call out the reserves that the mind might be clear to the last. Do we need to feed the sick for the purpose of keeping up the weight of the body generally and does feeding ever do it? Or is it the brain that most needs its structural integrity preserved, and can feeding do this if it cannot conserve the less important tissues? Can skeletons dictate wills that will stand law unless the brain is nourished think you?

Now, no sane person will ever maintain, that there can possibly be any pleasure in eating often during the day, when health has become so impaired that what and when to eat has come up for consideration. No one can say that food taken, even with indifference, ever gives any sense of refreshment, or that every mouthful taken when keen hunger comes does not send an electric thrill to the very finger ends. Is there not the very soundest philosophy behind all this, think you? And since no one can deny that so far as the brain is concerned it is entirely independent during emergencies of sickness of kitchen needs, do you not think it will do equally well during those morning fasts that may always be ended when hunger, relish and power to digest are duly evolved?

"But," says one, "if we wait until we get so hungry we are liable to eat too much." But you need not wait until you get famished, nor do you need to be run away with by a clamorous appetite. You are to exercise the virtue of self-restraint. But it may be said that a stomach that has gained power through a fast is in far better condition to handle a surplus than that stomach ever is to deal with even the lightest of lunches when there is no call from hunger.

This too is a case where mere statement ought to be argument, so exactly is it in line with experience. Can any deny that the mouth of hunger is full of water, full of relish, and the stomach alike eager to exercise its powers to add new life to body and soul; and since it is absolutely safe for brain reasons to let mouth and stomach get into this condition before eating, can any of you for one moment think it would be wise to adopt frequent feedings in time of ordinary health, or much less in time of indifferent or habitually poor appetite, or very much less to enforce food into the stomachs of the acutely sick? There is no danger that any of you will ever change your new way of taking your meals, for henceforward as long as you shall live you will find your forenoons so full of vital power, of vital energy, you will go through all the duties with such commanding ease and with such cheer of soul as will habitually keep you far above any temptation to tamper with food; in short, you will be no more tempted to eat during the morning hours than you will be tempted to the use of a cigar.

And there can be no more striking evidence of the soundness of the physiological basis of the dietary methods which I am trying to unfold than the fact that it begets such a degree of physical comfort that the accustomed cigar, or pipe, or glass of beer or whisky becomes an irritant and not a soother—there are no more any plaints to be soothed, do you not see?

Until we shall meet again ponder well these new points in "unwritten law," and as you ponder you will more and more clearly see that the morning luncheons are to be classed with the morning grog, the morning pipe or cigar.

LECTURE XIX.

THE FALL OF ADAM—LIFE A WARFARE—CASES OF ENLARGED WOMB AND DISEASE OF THE OVARIES—DRINKING AT MEALS—TEA AND COFFEE—THE TOBACCO HABITS—SHALL WATER BE TAKEN IN LARGE QUANTITIES WITHOUT THIRST?—NATURE'S POWER IN A VERY GRAVE DISEASE.

My Friends the Women:

I once somewhere chanced to read this couplet:

By Adam's fall,
We have sinned all.

This little couplet has two merits beyond question; it is putting a fact of belief in the easiest possible form to remember it, and it rhymes perfectly. The disposition to sin then, is an ancestral weakness, a born possibility with every human being that has the largest possibilities of development through culture. Hence everybody has something of the "old Adam" to arise and assume the mastery as the occasion occurs, and to hold him in due subjection is war.

Reverent hearts once had these words chiselled on the parental tombstone:

"Their warfare is ended."

In a most striking sense are our lives a continuous stirring up of those ancestral weaknesses, the "old Adam" possibilities that have been ours to inherit. It would seem that our lives are so full of strife through the goadings of our tastes and our needs, that it is warfare enough without being involved with ancestral complications.

But here is a note from one of you.

"Doctor,—I have a young lady friend, married, who has been in poor health for several years, and for a long time has been under treatment for an enlarged womb, and a disease of one ovary, but thus far with no favorable result. As she rarely has any sense of relish her meals are generally taken from a sense of necessity only. I easily see how your scheme may work in such a case, but she has been in poor health so long that she has become very despondent. Is there any hope of relief, when an ovary has been affected for a long time, through better nutrition?"

Signed, "A Believer."

I will give this note an illustrated answer.

A case came under my care in a young married woman, where an enlarged womb and a diseased ovary had been under special treatment for some three years, without avail. She had become so emaciated as to have almost a ghastly look. There was neither regularity of appetite, nor regular times of eating nor sleep, and local and general treatment had failed on these lines.

It was my first duty to take the husband, a R. R. trainman, into a course of culture. Possessing a very reasonable mind, I easily persuaded him that when he came home from his trips in the evenings or at night, the wife need not cook a general meal for him to take to his bed, and that when the call-boy aroused him in the night, the delicate wife might sleep on, for he himself, could get all the lunch the stomach ought to worry over, while the brain was weighted with the care of his train. With this reform promptly instituted, there soon came such luxury of nightly rest and sleep as had never been realized before, and in due time there was an appetite that never failed to be on time at about the same hour every day.

In less than six months there was added twenty pounds of **new woman,** and by so much, new spirit and soul. What about the ailings? They had nearly disappeared. And now for nearly three years this degree of health, this degree of relief, has been maintained with only such light relapses as have been invited by the sin of overdoing.

It was not necessary for me to know the actual condition of the womb and the ovary in this case, since there was no other human way to get relief, and had this failed then perhaps a surgical need would have been apparent. In this latter contingency the health-culture would all the better prepare the body for the surgeon's knife. Now, in this case, there was only martyrdom on the old lines of treatment. There is no way to lighten weighted wombs but through a better nourished body. There is no way to reach an ailing ovary, but by increasing the power of nutrition, except the extirpation of the surgeon's knife. The very highest art of modern treatment has been most persistently applied, and had to be given up because misery and not relief was the inevitable result.

It is a rule in surgery that there must be the best possible general condition before any grave operation is undertaken, hence, in all cases of ailing of pelvic or other organs or parts, there is great advantage in letting nature do all she can in preliminary treatment, and if she fails to fully relieve then there will be all the better condition for surgical work.

Now, I could not know how much of disease there was in this case, nor can it be known in any case, but I did know that because of the excessive general debility, there was an unduly weighted womb, and that there was a painful degree of trouble with an ovary; and I also knew that with the bad living habits, these local conditions could not but develop. Can you see then, what a satisfaction it is that one does not need to know all there is of disease in any case in order that all possible human aid shall be rendered?

"Give me a clear field," says nature, "and I will do all that can be done where the surgeon's knife is not required." I knew, that when this wreck of a young woman could get the normal exquisite sleep every night, and could have a keen appetite, with the daily living habits so guarded that there should be no undue taxing of vital power, disease, local or general, would have the best human chances for recovery. The clear field that nature wanted, was rest for the entire body at night, and for the day the best possible culture of digestive power that the normal weight and condition might be restored. This could only be by care not to get unduly fatigued, and not allowing the stomach to be called upon to deal with a surplus.

All this duly granted, nature went about her task, curing the sick places just as she would heal a broken bone; and the doctor could stand by with folded arms, and confident mien, for the work to be done was not for his profane hands.

I was never more impressed with nature's tireless energy in disease than in a recent case that came under my care. The patient had been troubled for many years with ailings in the region of the stomach. After a slow decline he finally came to his bed with symptoms that indicated catarrh of the stomach, due to possible ulcers. There seemed to be no other ailing. The rest-cure was applied and for a month there was no eating, nor could there be. Nature had locked up the stomach and kept the key in her own charge. By the aid of pain-relieving doses the stomach became quiet, the tongue became clean, but suddenly alarming mental conditions came on, that pointed to disease of the kidneys, and in a few days death came to end a disease that had been slowly developing two-score of years. The post-mortem revealed *healed ulcers* in the *stomach* and disease of both kidneys. Now nature went on doing all she could, and she did heal the ulcers in the stomach while the kidneys were getting ready for a fatal seizure upon the brain. Had there been a wound upon the body the healing would have gone on until the heart ceased to beat. We can always rely on nature doing all she can, if permitted to have her own way, and her work will be the very best that can be done. I once had an amputated finger nearly heal while the general condition was on the decline with death from lockjaw the inevitable—nature did all she could.

We are now ready to consider more questions.

"Doctor,—You have made it very clear to us that we can have the largest liberty in the spreading of our tables, but you have said little as to whether we may use tea or coffee as has been our wont, and with the same freedom that we use in the indulgence of our solids?"

Signed, "One of the Improved."

When I began my attack on the breakfast table many years ago I think I was wise to give tea and coffee a "wide berth." It was quite enough to try to abolish solids without even a hint that the "cup that cheers but does not inebriate" must also go. In my own experience I had found such infinite cheer from my morning cup of coffee, there was such a sense of power to do and to think, that I went on year after year with scarcely a thought of any evil as a result; it certainly was a very small evil compared with the breakfasts of former years. But in time I abandoned their regular use, holding them as a reserve for those times of exhaustion from professional strain that seemed always to invite ready-made cheer and physical energy. Their use habitually is a form of intemperance that inclines to cause "nervousness" and this is particularly true of coffee. Since I have become aware of the power of increased nutrition to lessen morbid wants, I have felt that for the greatest good for the greatest number a conservative course as to those drinks is the wiser way. Hence, when I can get the breakfast abolished there is an inevitable decline in the want of all stimulating drinks and for tobacco as well. A few months ago a business man who had "taken enough cod-liver oil to drown in," and who always felt the need of a cigar, even before he would arise from his meals, began the better way of living. It had been his custom to have a cigar almost constantly in his mouth during business hours. In a short time, almost unconsciously to himself, the habit was given up and why, and how?

Another man in active business began the higher life at about the same time and he has had to give up his between-meal beer and has also lost his appetite for tobacco, and why, and how? I will tell you: both of these men have become so well nourished, they feel such a perfect sense of comfort, that there is nothing to be soothed by either tobacco or beer, and hence their use has become somewhat an irritant in their effects. And so will tea and coffee go with those whose bodies become well and habitually nourished through stronger digestive powers.

I can very easily understand how the tea and coffee habit should be formed, but that the tobacco habit should be taken up in early youth, with the nervous system in perfect condition, and a disease deliberately invited, that makes the highest sense of comfort impossible, except drawn through a cigar, that such a habit should be deliberately formed when there is not the least sense of any want for its soothing effects, is a human anomaly. *No user of tobacco ever has the supremest use of his brain.*

Tea and coffee are exhaustive of the reserves of the brain, and hence in old age there cannot be the power of sustained thought where they have been habitually indulged. In these later years, when by virtue of a larger acceptance of my physiological conceptions of the science of living, I am moved to speak with more emphasis and freedom, I can but impress parents with the view that it is a physiological, hence a moral crime, to permit their children to use either tea or coffee, while I have no words to adequately condemn the culture that renders existence uncomfortable except when soothed by some form of tobacco.

What a storm of protests would there come from those youths who begin the habit because it is needed as an equipment for manliness, were all the young ladies to begin the public cigar and the home pipe or become experts in the art of "cud-turning and spittoon-spraying!" How many young men, contemplating homes of their own, would not be likely to estimate the possibilities of *cigars, tobacco, pipes, for two!* Women the weaker sex! Scarcely, when it comes to enduring all of life's irritations without artificial aid. Now, as to drinks at the table: you may set it down as a physiological fact that for the very highest reach of between-meal mental and physical felicity you must eat with such deliberation and thoroughness that you will not even care to drink, and you may be certain that if there comes physiological shortage of fluids, cool water only will be called for, or will fully satisfy.

Now for another question. "Doctor, what about drinking water for supposed needs when there is no thirst?"

Signed, "Inquirer."

Again I must ask you to put this down as a physiological fact, that for the highest possible mental and physical between-meal felicity, drink only as the need is indicated by thirst, and of course water that is both pure and palatable, and then avoid excess. There is an idea that large draughts of water flush out impurities as are the sewers flushed along the streets. The mouth rarely needs flushing except in a case of tobacco, nor does the channel that leads to the stomach; and as for your repeated glasses of water, they are at once absorbed into the blood only to be disposed of by evaporation through the skin, or more largely through the kidneys, and in both ways involving a needless tax that is not strengthening to the powers involved.

Here comes a very interesting question for consideration.

"Doctor,—I have a friend who has been a constant sufferer from too frequent calls to relieve the bladder, which has been an ailing since her last severe confinement two years ago. She complains that there is always a burning sensation that fails to ever become fully satisfied by the answer to the call. This has so broken up her hours of sleep that she has finally become one of the gloomiest and most hopeless of mortals."

Signed, "A Friend in Sympathy."

This trouble likely arose from an injury to the region of the outlet of the bladder. I had a typical case of this kind a few years ago, where the cause arose from the violence of a severe confinement. My patient was beyond sixty and had been a sufferer for twenty-seven years. She was a woman of powerful constitution and was able to endure all the remedies prescribed, patent and domestic, without becoming totally disabled. But at last she had gotten well into the Valley of Despair. There was always a burning sense of need of relief that called for frequent efforts. Sleep was greatly disturbed; the appetite had become nearly abolished, and a death was impending yet afar off that must come through a terrible conflict with nature, for there was a powerful constitution to be borne down. There was no disease except this most unfortunately located one.

There were the engorged vessels, a thin mucous membrane, whose nearly bared nerves were continually crying out for protection. It required only a few forenoons of fasting to restore the appetite of early years, and with it came an awakening of all the powers of being. The morbid calls became less frequent and the hours of disturbed sleep became further and further apart. Month after month the improvement went on, until within less than a year the normal condition was nearly restored. And this woman for more than eight years has been a most efficient homemaker for her aged husband and is still in active duty with no hint of her ancient trouble, though beyond her three-score and ten. How simple it all was! She had only to await hunger every day and immediately the dull pulses of being awoke with newness of life, and the bared mucous membrane, the nerves always on fire, the dilated blood-vessels, away out of reach of remedies, began to work with restorative energy. And in time the miracle of a cure was wrought and nature and not the doctor did it all. And this is only a marked case where there have been many lesser ones of the same character.

It would perhaps have taken years to bring the powerful constitution down to a merciful relief through death, and what a living death the years would have been!

Not only has this life been made comfortable for many years but a home has been restored that was wrecked; and more, such has been the impression made by the miracle that many others have been induced to adopt the "True Science of Living" to their great rejoicing over relief from various ills.

LECTURE XX.

ENFORCED FEEDING FURTHER CONSIDERED, WITH AN ILLUSTRATIVE CASE—EATING WHEN FATIGUED AN ERROR TO BE AVOIDED—MORNING HUNGER AND NATURAL HUNGER STILL MORE CLEARLY DEFINED—OLD AGE AND THE "NO-BREAKFAST PLAN"—A STRIKING LETTER FROM A RETURNED MISSIONARY.

My Friends the Women:

The statement is so often made by those who oppose the no-breakfast idea, who therefore have not tried the scheme and know nothing about the science or the sound physiology behind it, that it is better to eat often and less at a time, that I feel like enlarging still more on the matter of enforced eating. And all the more since on you falls the care of the sick. Indeed, if there is one subject that I may rightfully dwell upon over and over again, it is the grave matter of not feeding the well without hunger, and of not feeding the sick at all.

When I can get you to clearly understand how safe it is to stand by and over your sick, content to render to Nature's indications all that tender hearts and gentle hands can do, then will you become her handmaidens. A few years ago a tender wife gave her days and nights to the care of her husband low with a fever. Day after day, night after night she was compelled to enforce the prescribed rations of milk into a stomach kept paralyzed with dosings to allay pain, nervousness and to enforce stupor at night. At last after two months of enforced food with *no change of the bill of fare* the vital power became so (needlessly) exhausted that the mind was nearly reduced to chaos and then wifely hands had to enforce the dosings. The patient finally escaped with his life nearly a wreck, to be months in a slow approach toward the normal condition. Now the most strenuous advocate for the enforced feeding of the sick knows that milk, especially if reinforced with stimulants, could not be taken by the well, as a steady food for weeks without serious consequences. Where then, is the logic of feeding the sick on a food that cannot be borne by the well? Were the Samson of all living men to go on a diet of milk and stimulants only, there would result a debility that would slowly bring him to an invalid's bed and ultimately to death. Where then, is the logic of putting the sick on a diet that the well cannot endure without an immediate loss of power? No intellectual Samson is going to answer this question with physiological logic.

As it is a matter of daily anxiety with each of you to have some change of the bill of fare at every meal, just think for a moment of any *well* person going to a table three times a day and only finding one and the same article of food to satisfy hunger and for *two months!* Would not such an experience be likely to bring you to an invalid bed or chair? Would it not be very likely to so result if you were to sit down to those meals as often as for instance fever patients are compelled to take theirs? Can you have any doubt that this would be the result?

The old eating habits were resumed, but the previous health was not regained. There were some years of a disabled life when there was another "strike" and I was called to care for him. This time there was a combination of ailings that did not quite disable him, though there was such debility and languor that he required assistance in getting about his room. He was put on a rigid fast, water only being permitted to invade the sacred precincts of his stomach. It was a strange experience for the devoted wife, and but for the fact that I made her see that the patient was losing no strength as the days went on her heart would have failed her, for it was the first time she had ever had any conception that life could be sustained without food.

The third week of the fast was entered and with such increase of strength that he no longer required assistance in dressing and in getting down from his sleeping-room and in getting back to it. On the morning of the 18th day of the fast he bore upon his back a sturdy son of eight years as he walked downstairs to his sitting room. On the 19th day there was a hint of appetite and from thenceforward there was a relish for meals that recalled the young days when "life was fresh as the morning dew."

This man grew up on a farm, and when he became a brain-worker the old eating habits were kept up without a thought that he was habitually eating several times as much daily, in proportion to exercise, as he was when he spent long days in vigorous, fresh-air, general muscular labor; hence the invited strikes which duly and naturally occurred. Now all the while I was in attendance on this case there was serious apprehension on the part of his friends that the patient was doomed to die the death of hunger.

As the result of my attendance the patient not only made a rapid recovery from the acute disease, but has since had several months of growth into better health. And there is a woman whose kitchen has been emancipated from a full half of its former slavery; a woman who is grateful every day of her life for what the "True Science of Living" has done for her, and is doing to lessen her toils, and to ensure her family against the danger of sickness and of the common cruelties of sick-bed methods. With these two experiences her right arm will never again be strong enough to force food into stomachs where it can only be received with wrathful indignation.

A legal friend was an occasional witness to this miracle of nature as it went on, and he was confounded over what he saw, for to him death was inevitable. And he, too, has borne the "True Science of Living" into his own family, and there has come fresh life to all the members thereof.

Now as not one of you will ever eat a single meal so long as you shall live without hunger, I may well point out to you that for the highest health results, you must carefully guard against getting very tired before you sit down to your meals; guard well each day that there be only the least overdoing, because the account cannot be overdrawn without a full settlement, and one that will recall all the extra time made.

You who have your backs bent over washtubs every Monday morning, since you are certain to be driven by the "getting-through ambition," should make your first meals very light ones and much earlier than the ordinary, and when all is done then the whole body must rest, *rest,* and as the second meal is certain to come before there is rest in its fullness, it also should be light. You see the physiology behind the suggestion:—the stomach has a part in the taxing of excessive labor, and hence if you are to cut down its power you must also cut down its services.

You can have no conception of how important this is. You will begin to reflect when I tell you that for years I have made it a special object to ascertain the living habits of all the cases for which I have prescribed, and without any exceptions I have found avoidable cause the chief factor. True, there have always been the hereditary determining causes involved, but such, as I told you, are also matters of culture, Can you not easily see how far-reaching is this divine law in life? Not one of you but have suffered in some way as a direct result of avoidable violations. Some of you have had for years your bursting headaches, for which you have taken all the brain-paralyzers ever heard of, and so have lost the usual time of the attack with the added time of the recovery from the attacking drug, and only to find a steady increase in the number and severity of the attacks; and you have groaned in spirit that yours must be such unfortunate heads.

You will all find a rapidly developing need of studying your physical and mental limitations that your sins do not immediately find you out. And this will involve a great deal of culture in the grace of self-restraint, where there is the constantly arising temptation to put your hardest tasks through at any cost of muscle. The danger always lies in the fact that overwork, while it debilitates stomach-power, also creates the need of extra food that is usually manifest in the sensation of exhaustive hunger that food fails to relieve, except for a short time. There is a feeling of "too tired to eat, too hungry to wait for rest."

A question. "Doctor,—I find a great deal of opposition to the no-breakfast plan, because people do not understand that morning hunger is not real hunger, that it does not call in the most emphatic way for food, and for us who are going on in this new physical, and therefore spiritual Christianity, it is a little difficult to put our new ideas into very convincing language. That there is a decided difference between morning hunger and natural hunger is perhaps more easily realized than described. Will you please define the difference so that we who are laymen may always be ready to meet the inevitable, emphatic objection that I cannot do without my breakfast."

As I have told you, morning hunger is disease under culture; it is a matter so entirely generated by habit that it might just as well be cultivated to occur at any fixed hour, whether at two, three or four in the morning. It always is accompanied by a sense of exhaustion such as comes from undue mental or physical taxing. And it would be the same as a matter of cultivation, no matter when the hour. That this is a morbid condition is clearly evident without a resort to physiological proof, by the experience of thousands, that all hint of the unnatural feeling disappears, and very soon with most, after the habit is given up. This simply could not be if nature were being defrauded.

Now as to natural hunger, when it has been duly developed and without excessive muscle or brain taxing, the soul, the mind, every line of expression, in short the entire being, is radiant, as the attack on the first course of a well-ordered meal begins, and there is no hint of nerve exhaustion about it as the loaded table is approached. In your younger days before you knew overwork and the care that corrodes, you realized natural hunger as you never have since.

Morning hunger is behind the whisky habit and they who are its victims never are relieved from it day or night; there is always the exhaustion and the attending indescribable sense of mental and physical unrest that drives to the cup that muffles but does not cure the agonies of crucified nature. Now with your physiology and with your rapidly developing experiences, I expect you soon to become able to meet the most arrant skeptic on this subject with paralyzing power. I can say to you that with an experience of thousands of instances, I have yet to meet a single person who has seemed anxious to deny the reasonableness behind the method, thus showing that people are willing to accept new truth when it is placed before them so that they can clearly see and comprehend it.

In my own case the mere chance of taking a cup of coffee only, in an unusually severe attack of morning exhaustion, settled the question without argument, that more than this I did not need for the highest possible use of my powers during all the forenoon, no matter how severe the labor. Now breakfast was very suddenly abolished, and I accepted the forenoons with their comfort, their mental cheer, their physical energy, as a fact that needed no argument for their existence, even as the blind man accepted sight. And why not? I had been getting into a close approach to physical and mental wreckage, so close that all friends noted the progress and did not fail to remind me how badly I looked. Friends will do this you know, and with rarely any thought of how discouraging words will darken the soul. It is not very cheering to meet friends day after day, and after you have agreed on the state of the weather, to be told "how bad you look," and this was my usual greeting. But in less than a month color came to my face and energy to my expression, so that there were only greetings of surprise over improved looks.

So I began to teach others among the most needy, and always with the most striking results. During the many years that I have been teaching this "New Gospel of Health" I have often advised those who failed thoroughly to carry out the method, but they have been without exception deficient in will-power, too badly wrecked, or were natural gluttons, and hence the failure has always been one of deficient application of the means. In the dispensation of this higher method in life the sowing has often been on stony ground, on barren soil, but the science has never been unfolded to a single mind where there has been any power of reason, ***without conviction.***

One of your number asks whether I have any cases where the very old and broken down have found marked benefit from the radical change in living habits, I am very glad to have this question asked, because it is difficult for most people to comprehend that the change does not in some way involve a constitutional risk, hence the more light the better. In reply to this question I will read you an extract from a letter written by a returned missionary, and one of your sex:

"MY DEAR M. J.:

"I want to tell you of a new discovery in the laws of God which He is letting many of us make in these last days. It is what is known as the 'No-breakfast plan,' or the 'New Gospel of Health' as the writer, Dr. Dewey, calls it.

"We are commanded to 'prove all things; hold fast to that which is good,' So among many hundreds of others, our family has been proving or testing the 'No-breakfast plan.'

"I immediately left off my breakfast, taking my first meal about twelve or one o'clock, according to circumstances. My family looked on incredulously, but soon they saw such a marked improvement in me that one after another the whole family, lastly my mother (in November eighty-four years old), came on the plan.

"The improvement in each has been great, but most marked in mother, for twenty-five years superannuated through 'fatty degeneracy, and weak action of the heart,' for the past six or seven years she has been able to sit up her best days only from 1 P. M. to 8:30 P. M. Some days not up at all. Some days dressed to be up only two or three hours. When she renounced her breakfast, it consisted only of a tablespoonful of oatmeal and milk, or when her appetite was too low for that, three or four teaspoons of Mellin's Food for babies. Then we had to cater to a capricious appetite for dinner, and so for supper, which we forced upon her and which she crowded down in order to do what was right. Now that she has left off that mischievous breakfast-portion, she has found a hungry appetite and at midday she is ready for a considerable portion of whatever we have for dinner. *Anything* is relished; plain, hearty, or difficult of digestion, all seems equally suited. After the hearty meal she requires no more until next midday. She eats more at that one meal than she did at the previous three. Her waist-size has been reduced an eighth of a yard.

"She has suffered greatly the last six or seven years from her eyes and head, incapacitating her for needlework or reading, and when she was up you could see her most of the time leaning her head on one hand or the other. Now she is busy with some kind of light work from the time she is dressed until she retires, 9 P. M., and even 10 P. M.; some days even sitting a good part of the morning on the bedside, similarly occupied. Her muscular power was so gone that she could not preserve her balance to take *three* steps, always being rolled in an invalid's chair. Now she walks comfortably about the room. Her eyes are clear, laugh ringing and merry, intellect bright, and her soul has been much spiritualized. ***All this in two months.*** I should add that for the past eight years there has been no unaided action of the bowels, but after she had been on this plan for a month, there was a spontaneous effort of nature in this direction. I might detail the marked benefit that has come to each member of my family, to each differently, as the physical condition of each varied, but I must be brief. Oh had I known all this while I was a missionary in India there would have been I am sure, much more efficient years of labor.

"I cannot tell you how the Lord has blest me in the consideration that in thus eating and drinking I was doing it to the glory of God. And the increased mental and physical vigor has been gratefully returned to Him as so much more capital for Him to put out at interest for Himself. This plan is certainly hidden in God's Law as His method of sustaining life. Did you ever notice that when Jehovah-Jireh brought Israel, a nation of slaves, out of Egypt to train and develop them for himself, he gave for forty years, until the habit was well formed, but two meals a day, the first one *not* early in the morning? The manna could not be distinguished from dew, so they did not attempt to gather it until the dew was gone from the grass. It was light food and therefore required a large bulk to satisfy theeating of one person. It was the tiniest of all things, like hoar-frost on the ground, hence to gather for man, woman and child a sufficient quantity was a long task; then it had to be reduced to flour by the slow process of upper and nether millstone of the East, then to be baked or boiled. They could not have broken their fast before eleven or twelve M.

" 'Woe unto thee, O land, when thy princes eat in the *morning.*' Eccl. x. 16. The gain of the morning hours with God as a Christian and a Christian worker are inestimable. Oh had I known all this when in India as a foreign worker and missionary!

"Pray over it and see what God will show you.

"In best of bonds,
"Yours in Him,
"E. S."

You can thus see that even in extreme old age, and with disease involved, there can be no danger in a radical change of the living habits to a greater harmony with the laws of life. The older one is, the more debilitated, diseased, so is the need of a greater righteousness of living.

LECTURE XXI.

A CASE OF CULTURE IN OLD AGE—A SHORT DISCOURSE ON SKIN CULTURE—THE SCIENCE OF PREVENTION AS AFFECTING THE NEED OF PHYSICIANS—SLEEP CULTURE—A CLOSING VITAL SUGGESTION.

My Friends the Women:

Four months ago a man beyond 75 came to my office for some medicine for rheumatic knees. All his life he had been in wonderful health, never having had a single attack of acute disease since his childhood. His knees had troubled him for some years and had failed thus far to duly recognize the efficacy of drugs. Now this man, for his own good and for my advantage, had a logical mind, and although his stomach had never given him any trouble he was very easily made to see that his three hearty daily meals, with no exercise or business employment, were far in excess of the need as compared with the need from the very active exercise of his business life, hence he was easily persuaded to give up his morning meal. It was not however, so easy to persuade him that dosing was not needed for his rheumatic knees. This trouble was found to be a structural change due to excessive exposure and strain of the joints from his occupation of many years.

There has now been just four months of this higher life and he has lost entirely his morning want and he has gained the ability to walk easier than before, even without a cane ; a marked brightness of the eye, and a ruddy glow of the skin that extends to the hair on his forehead, and he has also gained a great deal of enthusiasm.

Now the effect of this higher nutrition on the skin is a good deal the same as is seen upon the grass when frequent warm showers come after a burning drought. In low nutrition, as I have told you, the vascular system is in a flabby state. We see in the face marked evidence of this, especially beneath the eyes where the veins are naturally weak; they become dilated, and hence their dark contents is revealed through the thin skin. These venous dilations throw the skin up in rough folds and the little arteries and the smaller arterioles which carry the bright red blood and lie deeper in the skin than the veins, become so covered that thereby the ruddy glow of the skin is lost and the retina by the toning up of all its structures becomes polished, hence clearer vision; and for a like change in the structure of the ear hearing is improved.

The first day of better living begins a change in the vascular system. The veins begin to tone down in size, the folds of the skin which would seem very large under a magnifier also begin to lessen; after a time, the arterial system becomes uncovered and hence a ruddy glow, a delicacy of tint and a plush-like softness of texture that needs to be seen with a cultured eye to be fully appreciated, but to the dullest of beholders the change is often strikingly observed.

Now you will all be glad to know that this method of living will clear any face of any kind of a skin disease that was not a born inheritance. It will relieve any diseases that have appeared on the skin after birth that are not malignant in character. Since two years ago I had occasion to advise for a homeless girl who was sheltered by her large-hearted friends, whose face was covered with blotches and pimples against which specifics had been launched for years in vain. She *listened* and went and did "likewise," and in a few months there was a ***natural skin.***

The eye glistens because the capillary, nutrient vessels, which carry only transparent blood, so tone up, that the white and the dark of the eye become condensed, polished, and the same effect taking place in the lens and contents of the eye chambers and the retina by the toning up of all its structures becomes polished, hence clearer vision, and with a like change in the structure of the ear, hearing is improved.

With men who use the razor this change in the texture of the skin becomes a matter of striking utility, in that it becomes so much firmer through the condensation, and the beard so much softer that it cuts with much more ease; you see that it is held in firmer grasp and being much softer because better nourished, the cutting conditions are all improved. A legal friend, during the last days of gluttonous living, took a razor that had become "villainously" dull to a barber for a new edge. A month after he had given up the soul-paralyzing morning meal, he called for his razor and received it from an assistant and on trial was well satisfied with the edge. Later on he met the barber, who apologized for not attending to this same razor which seemed to have sharpened itself!! The skin had become firm, the beard soft and hence the supposed better edge of the razor.

You easily see that this physical change must take place in the skin and the eye as a direct result of better nutrition, and hence you must see that it is the only rational way to meet the chronic, abnormal conditions found in disease of the skin. The application of medicated washes, and cerates, and ointments entirely fail to meet the structural needs of the curative processes; indeed there cannot be even an intelligent theory offered for their use. Their use, as well as the use of medicines in general, is founded on conceptions of needs that do not exist except in the imagination of the prescriber.

In the use of remedies I must duly remind you that we are always in a state of transition. It is within my own professional life that two of the most eminent physicians of my native state, strongly advocated a return to the bloody lancet as a chief means in the treatment of pneumonia! The lancet of a hundred years ago was the orthodox common means of dealing with acute disease, and that timid young physician would have been held guilty of malpractice who had failed to promptly use or who had failed to standby and see the purple stream of life flow long enough for the superstitious conceptions of his time! The lancet has become the memory of a barbarous, a bloody age in medicine. And, as the decades go on, so the orthodox treatments of the time become the barbarisms of the time to come. Means of relief change, but the structural changes by which cures take place or disease develops continue through all the centuries the same, the very same.

We are still in a superstitious age as to our conceptions of how nature cures. That she cures at all, is not to be inferred from our encyclopedias Materia Medica. Chemistry and pharmacy have done a great deal of refining in therapeutic art if not in science. We now have the active principle of medicines and not the nauseating bolus to swallow; all the same it is ever the cure by the means of dosage whether crude or refined and never the divine hand of nature.

A question. "Doctor,—Your scheme would almost seem to abolish the profession of medicine; how do you estimate the outlook of your profession when we all begin to live in harmony with natural law?"

Well I would have you all understand, in the clearest sense, that it is never absurdly proposed to have this higher method of living take the place of mechanics and the surgeon's knife in human ailings. Accidents will happen; children will be born who, by the hard lines of heredity must endure the martyr's day, months or years even under the best of conditions, only to die before the average limit of human life. And then there are the hard lines of environment, of fate by which human life is stifled in the countless overtaxings of mind, soul and body which fate hath deemed ***must come***. The "poor we have always with us," and the poverty of disease is still more universal. No, the office of the physician can never be abolished, with human life so involved with disease-inciting causes, avoidable or inevitable, and when it is yours to hover about the couch of your idol, you need one to lean upon, an earthly prop, as you cannot upon a higher source.

With the cure of disease so implanted in the mind as a matter of the skilled use of means and remedies, you will always need one whose large experience enables him to guide and interpret as you cannot for yourselves. It is mine to teach you not to become your own doctors and surgeons, but the science of prevention, the true science of living, by which you shall not only have more years added to your lives but that they shall be more abundantly filled with all that makes life worth living.

With the universal conception that disease always tends to death except when under the restraining power of special medication, dosing, domestic or professional, is to continue to be a mental if not a physical need, and they must continue to suffer most who are the least enlightened. In a higher sense you must consider your physician as a wise counselor in your time of trial, whose larger experience enables him to relieve your minds of needless apprehension, and to prepare you if the need must be, for the greatest of earthly sorrows. A worthy, educated and experienced physician ought to be one in every family group, and he should enter into homes with all the unselfish, friendly interests, that will enable him to do his utmost not only to relieve but to so enlighten as to lessen the future need of his services, even as he does in his own family.

In the times to come the science of prevention is to more and more displace the oblations, the offerings to the Moloch, disease, and as this science enlarges the proportion of physicians to the whole number of people, will gradually decline. I will close this lecture by the consideration of a question one of you is moved to ask.

Doctor,—Have you anything to say as to sleep culture?"

Yes, and a great deal might be said. You must fully understand from your own experience that excessive mental and physical fatigue interferes with refreshing sleep, hence it should be a law of your lives to habitually avoid excess in either way. Your beds should be soft enough to permit perfect relief from undue pressure, in other words, your beds should be in the highest degree comfortable during all seasons of the year. And then that your sleep shall be invigorating the air inhaled should be as fresh as if drawn from an open window. And one more suggestion, all subjects of a depressing character should be debarred as thieves and robbers from all sleeping-rooms. The mind should lose itself in sleep only in contemplation of the most pleasing of all human subjects. It has been my own rule for years to seize upon any subject that would give a little pleasurable tax to the mind as a sleep-persuader.

You may take this suggestion home with you to be so considered as to vivify it into life-long remembrance: the suggestion that if you are to keep your bodies in the strongest defensive condition against disease, you must cultivate and maintain the highest possible degree of physical and mental comfort; there must be the most comfortable existence during the day; there must be the most *perfect sleep* during the night.

LECTURE XXII.

OLD THEMES FRESHLY CONSIDERED—EVOLUTION OF EXHAUSTION OF FATIGUE—EVOLUTION OF REST, OF RE-CREATION—MORE REITER-ATION—ILLUSTRATIVE CASES—MISSIONARY WORK—SPREAD OF THE NEW GOSPEL—

My Friends the Women:

Has it ever occurred to you that the human body is subject to two very striking evolutions during every twenty-four hours? This is a most interesting and vitally important fact and cannot be too well understood by you whom it so much concerns. In unfolding it to you I shall only hold nature up in a little different light; we shall only reiterate something you already know but cannot know too well, for if there is one truth home-makers ought to know with absolute clearness, it is that the American breakfast is gluttony, is an abomination in the sight of Heaven, that cannot be too soon abolished.

On this one subject I am guilty of being a hobbyist of tireless persistence, and all the more since the evidence is coming in from the four corners of the earth that the giving up of this untimely meal is causing the greatest enthusiasm among all who are giving the scheme a fair test. And, since it concerns you homemakers more than all others that it should be abandoned, not only because your own lives will be strengthened in every way, but also for the immense advantage it will be to you all in an economic sense, I feel warranted in making another attempt to deepen the impression I have already made. And all the more since your voices are to be unceasingly heard as voices in the "wilderness"; and they must ring with the power of reason and persuasion.

You cannot too well understand the physiological reason there is against filling a human stomach in a body that has reached the maximum degree of rest and therefore of power, to endure several hours of the severest mental and physical labor, of power that works with vastly more ease than when not influenced by digestive energy. In your walks in the "wilderness" you shall need neither "purse nor scrip," but you shall continue to need countenances aglow with health, the most enlightened intelligence and a moral earnestness and persistence that shall be all-abounding.

If I were to ask you when one is in the best possible condition for a hard mental or physical task, you would at once say that it was when the body and mind are in the highest degree of rest. Now when is this condition reached in the daily experience of human living? Let us consider. When one in perfect health involuntarily opens his eyes at the end of a night of sleep it is because rest has done its most perfect work. There then begins, even with the very slightest voluntary movement, with every thought or emotion, an evolution of fatigue, an evolution in which the destructive forces that affect molecular life and that go ceaselessly on during life, are to exceed the constructive forces and the excess will be in exact accord with mental or physical activity. With those engaged in very heavy manual labor, a state of exhaustion may be reached. This evolution goes on until sleep becomes the one supreme object of earthly desire, and when finally all restless turning is ended and the eyes close in sleep the maximum degree of fatigue is reached and from thence there is the evolution of rest, of regeneration, that goes steadily on through all the hours of night until the body has been restored to its normal balance.

Now I want to ask you, if you accept as a fact the evolution of rest through sleep, why you are not in the best condition to begin your days of toil as soon as you are duly appareled for them? You are never hungry at the waking hour, for there has nothing been done to make you hungry, and you know when there is no hunger there is no sense of relish, there has been no call for any special kinds of food; the mouth glands are torpid, so also the glands of the stomach; in short there is entire absence of digestive conditions. Now if you really are in the highest possible condition of rest when your eyes first open of their own volition in the morning, what more absurd thing can you be guilty of than to put food into your stomachs before you begin your daily toils or before you have duly created a need by the activities of your labors?

Can it be other than to make use of the stomach as a vehicle to conveniently carry food about *before* it is needed? Now that you have lost that morbid morning want, now that you have found that it actually requires several hours of active exercise to draw off the accumulated strength of the night of sleep, hours of keener intellect and of greater muscular energy than you have ever realized before, you wonder and wonder again over the gluttony of the American breakfast.

You have now been living quite long enough on this truly physiological plan of life, to begin to have a definite conception of its vast meaning for the world's workers. And the more you think of it the more you wonder over its simplicity. Now what is it not worth to a mortal man or woman to be able to arise in the morning with a feeling that there need be no thought or care about the health, that the labors of the day can be entered upon, and that nature will be at her best every way considered, while the empty stomach is gaining power to handle the relished, refreshing meal; that during this morning fast, nature will be at her best, not only to ward off disease, to cure disease, but to maintain the health of body, soul and spirit!

I often say to people that they are not getting sick when they are on the road to hunger, and the assertion always makes a strong impression on an intelligent mind. The world is full of text books on health culture, but they all teach systems that involve a great deal of doing, especially for the health, of thoughts about the health, that are inevitably given up because of their taxing power upon time and patience, and then there is lost all the good that resulted. They have all been written without any conception of the wonderful power of the brain to feed itself for days and weeks, with absolute safety to health, and therefore they all enjoin methods of diet based upon the supposed need of feeding regardless of the want of appetite, to keep up the strength. As you go on in this new natural way of living you will more and more wonder that this wonderful power of the brain has remained a hidden truth through all the ages.

Can you ask for anything more simple than a plan of living that gives the highest health, and therefore the greatest mental strength and cheer to the mind without the least taxing effort? You arise in the morning now, knowing that you are at your best for any of your life's duties; you give your sole attention to them and, wonderful conception, while the fasting hours go on, not only are you at your best, but nature is at her best in ability to go on and cure those diseases that have been under culture for years. While you are getting hungry the cause behind the headache is slowly disappearing; the cause behind the nasal or bronchial catarrh is slowly disappearing, and only think, those who by debility have suffered long with woman's peculiar ailings have every assurance that all of them not requiring the surgeon's knife, are most rapidly improving when vital power is not being taxed with a meal taken several hours before it is needed.

Again I must assure you that morning hunger is disease under culture, and that the cure can only come by giving up the morning meal fully and finally, and when once the "dying pangs" of this life-long bad habit are finally stilled, the morning hours will be the brightest for what is to be done. Can you ask for anything more simple, available, effective? Just think again what life must be, when there can be those mornings of comfort with the very largest assurance that there need be no fear of an attack of disease, and that your old chronic ailings, punishments for sins daily repeated, are all under a process of expiation and with the largest hopes of complete remission!

When you realize in largest measure what this divine ordinance means for suffering humanity, then you will enter upon a ministry that you will never resign while you are capable of feeling for the woes of others.

The very simplicity of the means, the rapidity with which favorable relieving results are realized, makes it an easy gospel to teach. And once you get a vivid sense of a healthful life, you begin to see that morning meals are gluttony, *suicide,* and hence can you other than stretch forth your helping hands and lead your friends out of danger?

And then the results are so far-reaching. A few months ago one of the first citizens of a great city who chanced to pick up the "True Science of Living" in a bookstore, found in the introduction by Dr. Pentecost, a history of his own headaches. For forty years he had been afflicted with sick headaches not less than once every month, and in recent years a throat catarrh had developed that was so annoying at night that several handkerchiefs were kept in easy reach. And there was a degree of habitual indigestion for which he always carried a vial of laxative pellets and soda lozenges.

He read the book and at once postponed his first meal until the usual luncheon time. The result has been that during three months there have been no headaches; the catarrh is nearly relieved, and he has found no need to be a perambulating drugstore. Now this "New Gospel of Health" through him, has gone from one friend to another, each taking it up, vitalizing it, and imparting it to other friends. And so is the science of living going through a great city.

With such results to relate, you will deal leniently with my tendency to reiteration. It was repeatedly charged against Wm. Lloyd Garrison that he talked too loud and too unceasingly, but there was one who said of him that he was talking to deaf people. Is there greater slavery to talk against than the universal slavery of self-welded bonds of disease? Is there slavery more universal? Why shall we not cry out till "the dead in sin shall awaken?"

Since nature in all cases has to do the curing, how safe it will be for you to advise your friends, and how pleasurable it will be when you know that the change you shall advise will give all the ailing ones a longer lease of life even where those ailings are beyond cure! Perhaps consumption will have its victim in its fatal, withering grasp, that grasp must relax somewhat when the power of nutrition is raised by meals adjusted to periods of hunger. Perhaps it is a case of organic disease of the heart; there will come some relief that will add freshness to the breath of life; perhaps it is a case of cancer; if you can interpose between the dying patient and all unbidden meals, there will be something of comfort added and therefore a lengthening of days.

It is a new conception with all of you, that in all cases nature is continually warring against adverse conditions to prolong every human life to its natural limit. She is at work as industriously to this end in cases as inevitably fatal as in the most trivial, and all she asks at your hands is that you shall not make her industrious hands heavier with your heavy hands. In all cases, no matter how slow the course, whether of cancer or consumption, food will be called for as needed and it will be used with life-sustaining effect, *if wisely taken.* You cannot possibly over-estimate this fact in its vital meaning, that indifference or aversion to food is an exact measure of the inability to duly digest and assimilate and therefore the danger of subjecting vital power with the needless tax of disposing it.

With the light you now have, each of you will become a power of good to all your suffering friends. Knowing that no death can ever occur from mere starvation until the skeleton condition is reached—a condition that in many would require nearly three months of brain-feeding—you can enter all homes and cry out against unbidden food as a crime that involves death in its tendency. You may now go to your homes with the great thought that henceforward it must be yours to let your light shine upon all the dark ways of *unrecognized-man-woman youth-and-infancy-slaughter.*

LECTURE XXIII.

HYGIENE OF PREGNANCY—ETHICS OF THE FAMILY RELATION—MORNING SICKNESS—EMOTIONAL INSANTIY—A FRESH ILLUSTRATION OF NATURE'S POWER IN CASES OF EMERGENCY—ILLUSTRATIVE CAS-

ES—PROF. CHAS. MILTON BUCHANAN, M.D., ON ANTISEPSIS AND GERMI-CIDES.

My Friends the Women:

I am now to begin a special course of lectures of an advisory character that will involve very little that will be new to you physiologically.

My first topic will be about the care of your lives during pregnancy. What it is to a man and a woman to be bound to each other in equal relation to a human life in its most dependent, helpless stage of existence, is one of the most inviting themes for thought and reflection to the moralist. I have no voice or pen to portray what it has been to me to realize that there has been one woman and three young lives solely dependent upon my care and toils, for all that has made life of worth to them, nor what of life it has been to me to have the abiding inspiration of their needs and their affection.

I know nothing so drear in all human experience as a midnight ride in the country in the winter season. The darkness, the silence, the gloom, with all nature cold in a seeming death beyond resurrection, all tend to make one feel that he alone is left of all the living. During such hours how inspiring, warming has been the thought of the peaceful sleepers at home, how elevating to the soul to do, to suffer and to endure, as in the gloom of a graveyard, that they might have more of life. A human life to reach its highest perfection, must habitually realize the happiness of caring for the dependent ones, of living for them. The only complete home, the only perfect life, is where there is the father and the mother, the sons and the daughters; and that marriage falls far short of the divine idea where there are no children to cultivate the heavenly graces of self-sacrifice.

The human soul reaches its loftiest heights in doing for others, and a growing family furnishes its natural opportunities in the greatest degree. I was never more impressed with this, than when a few years ago the head of a great plant, in agony from an assassin's bullet, first thought, not of revenge, but of his aged mother and of the shock and the pain his wound would be to her. Is not such a relation Christ-like in its ennobling influences? Here was one of the world's giants in business, but the thought of the mother makes him only a great human boy, still dependent on that affection that only a mother can inspire.

As my lectures deal only with matters of a practical nature I cannot enter into any consideration of the fitness of the marriage relation as between individuals, with reference to the implanting of hereditary-tendencies to disease, moral, mental or physical in new lives. Love is said to be blind, unreasoning; it is certain she will have her own way, and her ways are often wonderfully mysterious, unreasonable to those interested, but who look on with eyes unblinded, with hearts untouched by emotional insanity. Can love see anything? Not with the philosophic vision of interested friends. Your sons and your daughters will marry, not regardless of your preferences, but unhindered by them, and by social, moral, mental, physical, pecuniary or any other consideration. We are compelled to accept this as a fact, over which we may moralize but we shall not make the blind see with our eyes. And so it seems inevitable that the world will go on in the same old way in its marrying, and giving in marriage, and without the shadow of hope that attachments will ever originate in the head and not in the heart.

We now come to the question of what the living habits shall be during pregnancy. In a general way they should be the same as in the ordinary condition, only there should be all the care possible to have the surroundings of the greatest possible cheer. Since vital power is to be taxed with the maintenance of one body, and the building up of a new one, she should have every possible advantage in her work. The pregnant woman should have every possible cheer added to her life, and it should be relieved of all possible taxing care or taxing labor, in short, it is the duty of all within her home circle to treat her with the very largest consideration.

Pregnancy is often a period of emotional insanity, of the most unreasonable conceptions and actions. Women at times accuse innocent parties of the grossest immoralities. I myself, was once so accused, and but for the fact that the husband in whose family I had been the trusted physician for years was not a hot-head, I might have fallen the innocent victim of an assassin's rage. In due time there was developed a degree of mental obliquity that most amply cleared the atmosphere of all moral deficiency.

I must call your attention to only one ailing of pregnancy and this, that monstrous one, morning sickness. This is one of those mysterious ailings that seems for once to put nature in a gross fault. That when food needs to be taken, not only to maintain one's life but to build up a new one, that it should be refused with scorn seems nothing less than an anomaly, past all finding out, a mystery in nature's human affairs, deep, inexplicable.

But how are we to deal with this willfulness? Up to the present time Nature has refused ever to be placated in the least with all means of human devising! The materia medica has been ransacked over and over again for peace-offerings, only to be refused with imperial disdain.

What is morning sickness? My answer is that it is a morning protest against putting food into a morning stomach. What is the cause of it? *I don't know*. How is it to be treated? Is it safe, you feel like asking, not to feed when there is a double need for the digestion of food? Is it any good, think you, to put food into a stomach when it is to be ejected with indignation? I say no, emphatically. There have been cases where there is such habitual irritability of the stomach during the entire period of pregnancy, that nearly every meal was ejected, and yet with normal confinements and the birth of well-developed infants.

I had a case many years ago where the constitution was unusually delicate, and the acquired debility was so great as to make drawing the breath of life laborious. Only one meal could be taken daily and this late in the morning, and it seemed to lie in the stomach until late at night, as a mass undergoing slow combustion. The confinement was one of the easiest, and a sturdy male child was born that grew up to a stalwart manhood remarkably free from ordinary human ailings, to become an agriculturist of unusual brawn. But his unborn life called nearly all of his mother's reserves.

I have had no cases of morning vomiting where there were no unbidden morning meals, and why should I have? If no breakfasts are put ***down into*** sick stomachs no breakfasts will be thrown ***up out*** of sick stomachs. If no luncheons or dinners are put into sick stomachs there will be none ejected with righteous indignation. A sick stomach is a stomach that needs to be retired from active service and put on an unlimited furlough, and with absolute faith that it will report for duty with lofty patriotism when ready for action. Putting food into sick stomachs is as void of sense as anything that ever occurs outside of homes for the feeble-minded.

During the present year I had the care of a woman in the last months of her pregnancy, whose constitution was delicate and whose condition, apparently, became very grave during the last weeks. The abdominal enlargement became unusually great, and the feet and limbs became distended to almost the bursting condition through a dropsical effusion; all color departed from the skin; there was no real rest day or night, and rarely any normal sleep; the appetite was such that long fasts were required to develop hunger. It was the most taxing case of human endurance I ever had charge of. With my "mind's eye" I saw only thin muscle floating in water; the fat all gone as brain food, and for the building up of the unborn life within. Was there disease involved? How many times would this query come with startling, portentous force?

The hardest of all professional experiences is to see a young family deprived of that tender, tireless care that only a mother can give; to see a home wrecked, the children scattered by the cold, relentless hand of death. This delicate woman so heavily weighted as to scarcely be able to be about, became the mother of two well-developed infants, but there were four or five days spent, apparently on the border land of life, after nature's supreme effort. There was no eating, but there was a rushing back of the waters into the vessels; the brain still had some reserves to draw upon. These were kindly given up to the emergent needs, until the rested stomach began to speak, and then with the waters all absorbed there began a vigorous return towards the normal condition in weight, strength, etc.

Is it not strange that two unusually strong, well-developed infants were born in this case? It was even so, but they cost the mother nearly all the reserve tissue she had left to accomplish the miracle. They left enough, you see, to keep the brain from starving until the digestive machinery could rest into power to run for *three lives.* A miracle this? Nothing less. You may well think so when I tell you that during the last weeks before the confinement this woman did not eat enough to keep her own body in the normal condition, and so her own brain and those growing bodies had to rely on what her body could spare, but they drew her very nearly to the "dead line."

You can now understand, as you have not before, how it is that well-developed, strong infants can be born when the mothers are in the last stages of consumption or other wasting diseases. This involves the miracle of a dissolving of tissues that can be spared, and their absorption into the blood, that every need of the unborn child shall be met. You will now see that there can be no need to eat for two, or even three during the months of pregnancy, when it cannot be done with relish. There is no reason whatever for enforced meals, any more than in the ordinary condition. A sick stomach is no more able to work than a sick wood-chopper, and there can be no more rational way devised for the relief of morning sickness than to *starve it out.*

The months of pregnancy ought to be of the utmost cheer and of the largest avoidance of all mental and physical taxing. Each day should be a life, in itself, to be made the most of, in all that can add strength and cheer existence. The confinement should be considered an event which must be met with all the physical powers in a state of highest efficiency. This involves regularity in all living habits. The work of the hands must not excessively fatigue; there must be regular hunger and all the sleep necessary for complete rest.

In the last weeks when getting about begins to be laborious, there must be extra care that eating is not in excess, and if the bowels for this reason become sluggish, the movements must be aided, not with drugs, but with warm water flushing. There will be no need to discriminate against the sense of relish in any meal during the entire pregnancy and if those meals are taken as they should be, the bill of fare for each maybe as varied as the relishing sense may indicate. Every day should be a contribution to health that there may be the highest possible defensive condition against the attacks of disease on the day of confinement.

I will close my lecture by reading some extracts from a little work on Antispasis and Antiseptics, by Professor Chas. Milton Buchanan, of the National University of Washington, D. C, that are very much in line with the last suggestion I have made, in line with the basic idea of every lecture I have delivered before you, and I rejoice exceedingly that I have chanced to find authority so recent, so corroborative, so emphatic.

"Undoubtedly the greatest of all antiseptics and germicides is health. It is only when the natural and normal efficiency is vitiated that Nature becomes dependent upon Art. The healthy tissues of the human body neither harbor infectious organisms nor favor or aid their subsequent development when introduced. Indeed there cannot now be the slightest doubt but that the highest type of histologic vitality, which we commonly term health, is highly prejudicial to the action of pathogenic bacteria. Furthermore when such have been introduced within the system, either by accident or design, they are quickly destroyed either in the circulation or tissues, or else discharged through the various emunctory channels. Cunningham and others have proven that bacteria are frequently destroyed in the blood; Vaughan too has demonstrated the germicidal power of the nuclein of blood-serum. . . . The medical literature of the past few years contains many references to the germicidal properties of blood-serum. . . . So it seems that all of the normal functions of the body work together for its good in the preservation of its hygienic and vital activity. When we consider how slight a cause may interrupt the normal operations of this delicate and highly complex machine called the human organism, how careful and watchful of its health we should be. These natural conditions and beneficent tendencies of the organism may be perverted by various causes such as injury, cold, inflammation, embolism, local or general depression of vitality, etc. For centuries men have climbed mountains, crossed oceans, bridged chasms, delved into the bowels of the earth, burned the midnight oil, courted death in a thousand forms in a vain and endless search for the illusive and delusive "Elixir of Life." All this time they labored in ignorance of the fact that the treasure sought lay constantly within their reach—nay, more—pulsing through their very beings. And yet—and yet—they found it not."

Ah Professor, if you believe that rich blood is the true Elixir of Life, that good health is the best defense against the terrible microbe, then should you not believe that disease is a condition that cannot be logically attacked by the antiseptics of chemistry? Will it not be better for all people to believe that disease is a matter of life-long culture through bad living habits, largely avoidable, of which the attack is a legitimate summing up, rather than a riotous disturbance of myriads of microbes who have by chance become in possession of the very citadel of life?

Is it absolutely certain, Professor, that the success of modern surgery is wholly due to the germ-destroyer and not in part to better hygienic methods in the details of operations, certain that success in surgery has become conspicuously greater in a comparative sense, than success in the treatment of disease? Is it absolutely beyond all question that vaccination has caused a decline in prevalence and fatality of smallpox, conspicuously greater than has been in other diseases, as typhoid, typhus fevers and other common diseases that have not been subjected to specific, extraordinary preventives?

My friends, I wish you to remember every one of the words I have read, for nothing I have said to you is more important since it falls upon you as mothers, to so care for your children that they shall always be in the best possible condition to defend themselves against the bacillus of diphtheria, of scarlet fever, etc., and all the more since you may have little time to get the blood rich enough to *save* in malignant cases.

LECTURE XXIV.

THE MICROBE AGAIN—THE LYING-IN ROOM AND THE REST CURE— BILLS OF FARE DURING THE DAYS OF CONFINEMENT—IRRIGATIONS

CONSIDERED—CARE OF THE BOWELS—STRENGTH CULTURE—CARE OF THE NEW-BRON BABY—SHALL IT BE BATHED DAILY—HOW IT SHALL BE NURSED—NIGHT NURSIND CONSIDERED.

My Friends the Women:

In these modern times when portentous microbes are being marshaled in hordes, each an energetic, virulent "enemy of souls," the lying-in room thereby has become invested with a new danger, until parturient involution is becoming more and more a marked process and less a physiological sequence. This is particularly the case in the cultured medical centers, where the largest consideration is given to the minutest details of lying-in service.

During the many years I have been engaged in such services I have become impressed with the importance of relieving the mind of all apprehension of its being any other than one of the most natural of nature's processes and involving only the slightest danger of complications through "attacks" of disease. The throes of agony, the days of prostration, of invalidism are quite enough to anticipate during the long months, without having the lying-in invested with undue solemn attention to a surplus of details.

As to what is to be done or not done during the throes of labor, that must be left to you, and your medical attendant. It is mine to advise what shall be done after your agony is over. That all calls of congratulation shall be excluded until you have so far regained strength as to find it necessary to see the most cherished friends is a matter whose importance only need be stated.

The lying-in room must not be considered a monk's cell, but rather a room that must be lighted not only by the sun that shines in the firmament, but also by the sun that shines in the soul of a friend. "Blessed is the single heart that comes to us in need." Only the wise friend, the friend that has power to bring the cheer from without to relieve the tension of the long days within shall be admitted. The lying-in room has need to be kept free, Hot only from the monk's cell sense, but also from the prisoner's cell sense, hence friendly calls that cheer without taxing are clearly admissible, and all the more if your trained nurse is an uninteresting personality. It will be all the safer for you to have your lying-in rooms relieved with social cheer, because your eating habits will be physiologically adjusted, and hence there will only be the least danger of an attack of disease through the cheer that comes with the call of a friend.

The agony over and your beds made as comfortable in every way as human hands can make them, rest becomes the supreme need, and that rest may be as perfect as possible. You are permitted to turn or move, or be moved in any way that will relieve the tension of a fixed position. In older times when lying-in rooms were more largely in the hands of the barbarism of an uneducated midwifery, hapless women were compelled to lie for hours on the back with unchanged bedding, not daring to relieve the tension by a change of position.

You are going to rest for hours, days or even weeks, as the need shall be, and that it shall be as perfect as possible, the body and the mind must be kept in the largest possible degree of comfort. As you are to be cut off from fresh air, hunger-inciting exercise for many days, you will not take that first meal until you can relish it as a belated picnic dinner, and because you will only take the least exercise, you will not relish or require more than one meal daily; does this look like starvation? Think a moment: Will not your muscular exercise be cut down more than one-third? Why not then cut the meals down as much?

A question reaches me at this point that seems to require a reconsideration of bills of fare. "Doctor,—Do you really have no special diet scale for the lying-in room?" In reply I must again suggest that bills of fare are arranged on geographical lines. Were my audience made up of representatives of nations, I would have need to say to Madame of the South Sea Islands, "You will only partake of your breadfruit as hunger indicates whether once every day or once every week." To Madame, the Esquimaux, "Not quite so much blubber every day as when you are busy about your ice-hut." To Madame the "Almond-eyed," "Have your rice, but be very certain you want it before you ask for it."

You must fully understand that Nature did not intend that the lying-in room should be a sick-room, hence there is no reason for any special change of diet. Were a stalwart, a wielder of the axe from the Maine woods, to go into his bed in perfect health, to remain for many days, you at once see that such an infinite cutting down of his vigorous exercise would necessitate a corresponding cutting down of his bill-of-fare. And as you are to keep in mind that while you are in bed somewhat weakened by the lessened exercise of the last weeks of the pregnancy and still more by the throes of labor, and the general muscular inactivity that follows, there must be a wise adjustment of the times of eating.

There is no truth I have uttered in these morning lectures that I would press home to you with more force than that wonderful and unspeakably important physiological fact that when there is to be a battle with disease, Nature wills that there shall be no battle in the stomach and bowels over unbidden meals. You cannot too clearly understand that the lying-in woman is never so safe from the attacks of disease, is never in such perfect condition for recovery, no matter what the ailing, as when the stomach and bowels are in a state of ***absolute repose,*** quietly resting into power of vigorous action when the signal shall come. This is a physiological truth that ought to be proclaimed from the top of every ice-hut, house, palace, thatched shanty that is occupied by man, woman or child. Nature never makes any mistakes as to her needs when her voice can be heard.

What about daily irrigations, holding in solution the germ-killer? Shall you be annoyed with their daily use? With a thunder-bolt emphasis I must say No. Let me restate something I gave in a former lecture. In all parts denuded, whether by nature or violence, there is rapidly thrown out a slimy covering, a defensive coat of mail that is their own sure protection against septic absorption: this covering is thrown out to ***remain*** so long as needed and not to be ***removed*** by irrigation. As for parts not abraded they have all the needed power of self-protection.

In cases of cancer of the womb, the vagina will carry the foetid discharge for months without itself becoming diseased or without septic absorption that might mercifully paralyze vital power and suddenly end a living death.

In the city of my home there have been two midwives, one of whom had for years a far larger obstetric practice in lying-in cases than any competing physician ever had, and the other, her successor, also had a practice that led by a good deal her gentlemen and lady competitors. Neither of these understood the simplest principle of scientific treatment or care, and yet they never seemed to have any fatalities due to septic absorption. One of these never permitted the bed to be relieved from contamination until after hours of motionless, torturing existence. There is a woman now living who has attended most of the cases that have occurred in a large country neighborhood in fifty years and without a *single fatality.*

Child-bed fever can never occur except it has been under culture for months or years even, and when the condition has reached its fullness, the lying-in will be the occasion for the outbreak and there will be no time for defense, for nature will be disarmed; and medicated irrigations cannot enrich the blood, enrich as Professor Buchanan would have it, to be the abiding, the chiefest of all germ destroyers.

During thirty years of very considerable obstetric work, I have never annoyed a single patient with irrigations, and not a single death from septic causes.

What about the bowels? Shall the traditional dose of physic be given on the second day? Perhaps, if there has been eating right along regardless of condition or times, if there is to be the usual three daily eatings while in bed. In this case the bowels will need to be relieved perhaps frequently from the strife within over the disposal of food mass in a state of decomposition. But with all who have come down to the lying-in couch in that high physiological condition that is reached through due obedience, and who are to remain in line with Nature during all the days of enforced repose, the bowels may be left alone to make known their own needs and when there is a hint of want there may be a flushing with warm water if necessary. This physiological way is not only absolutely safe but it saves from the loss of a day or two of growth into strength, through the prostration of the powers from bowel scourgings.

Since the lying-in condition is not one of disease any more than the pregnant condition, the traditional nine days on the back demands a consideration. As soon as the first complete rest from the exhaustion of the labor has been reached, muscle culture may begin. There may be all the freedom of movement on the bed that the lower abdomen will permit without any complaint. When the tenderness is all relieved, getting into an arm-chair or on a couch when there are strong arms to relieve any taxing self-exertion, is very restful. There should be no taxing, sudden efforts and all muscular exertion should come short of the fatiguing sense. Day by day must strength be added to strength until the normal power is regained.

The very essence of the care of the sick or disabled may be condensed as follows: Keep the mind in the greatest possible cheer; keep the body in the greatest possible comfort; relieve tired, aching muscles and joints by massage and passive exercise; assuage thirst with pure, cool water; keep the body and bed duly clean; listen to all of Nature's plaints, do all you can to soothe them and she will do the rest.

What about that infant, the first-born perhaps, that jewel of priceless value upon whose sleeping face you gaze, hour after hour, beside which all else in the wide, wide world dwindles into insignificance! To begin, having been duly made clean, and appareled in the cleanest of clothes, it is to be kept in the cleanest, in the most comfortable, of all human situations, its delicate skin is not going to get so soiled as to require soap, towels and flesh-brush, for at least one whole week. Nor will your own particular heart's idol during all the months of its tenderest care, need its general bath more frequently. Why should it, when, by virtue of its inestimable worth, you will keep it so cleanly appareled?

The first important question to be met in this new life that is so helpless, so dependent, is the one of feeding. Usually its own natural supply is withheld for two or three days and even more, and what then? You will now understand what it is to **know** that your jewel also has its storage of brain-food, that will duly keep the vital powers in motion far better the while than can be done with the tough curds from the milk of the farm-yard. You had a great deal better permit your idol to cry with an empty stomach when it will not be attended with spasms of agony, with a drawing-up of the limbs because of a combat over green cheese in the helpless bowels. For a whole week dairy milk must be deemed a last resort, by which time the maternal supply will be available, if at all.

How often shall the babe be nursed? I want to tell you, with all due emphasis, with all due solemnity, that from the beginning to the end of the nursing months of its life, if you feed your babe more than four times in twenty-four hours, if these times are regulated by cryings and not by regular periods, you will by so much make possible a discharge of your nurse, to be succeeded by the **undertaker.** And these words might be rightfully chiseled on the headstone, "Died from the ignorance of its mother!" Such an epitaph might well be chiseled on a frightful per cent. of the smaller headstones, that fairly spangle our cemeteries.

Now to get down to the practical consideration of this vital question. The first thing you should do every morning after you have appareled yourself is to nurse your child. The last thing you should do before entering your beds at night is to nurse your child, and that should be the last nursing until the next morning. Between these nursings the periods should be closely regulated by time. With the bodily exercise of a child very little, and scarcely varying during the days of the first year of existence, there can only be the least variation in the amounts required at each meal, hence, in the largest degree, hunger can be regulated by the clock. There is a most striking advantage in this limited, regular number of feedings in that, when, as often occurs, the maternal supply fails, hunger being perfectly natural, there will be a failure to fully satisfy, hence there can be brought into use artificial supply, to make up the loss, this increasing as the natural fails.

It is my experience that regulated, limited feedings prevent all morbid sense of hunger and give to babyhood the highest possible chance for life. A worrying child is always by so much a sick child; it is never cross except from the wrath of indigestion. With meals exactly regulated it is one of the most comfortable of mortals until a very near approach to the feeding **moment**.

As for night-nursing it is entirely a matter of habit and a very bad one. There is absolutely no physiological need and a night of rest is no less important for the tender life than for the mother. If the habit has become formed it should always be broken and it will require only a short time in most cases. With perfectly regulated meals there is the largest assurance of safety, against the danger of cholera infantum, of diphtheria, in short, against all the dangers that threaten the sacred precincts of the crib.

I may remind you in passing that in order that the babe shall have perfect sleep it should always sleep alone, hard by you, but not with you. This will insure regulated temperature all through the night. When you are compelled to resort to artificial food particularly to store hoard milk, all the more will this regularity be needful, and all the feedings should be with exceeding slowness, that the stomach shall have to deal with particles and not masses. And when these have to be dealt with I am fully persuaded that there will be more power over them with only three feedings instead of four. No infant can starve or fail to fully develop on ***three full daily meals***. During the first year of infantile life there needs to be the greatest care that the body should be so dressed that there shall be maintained an average normal temperature.

With these exact feedings you will not have on the average more than one bowel movement per day of fine yellow paste, void of all curd particles, and when there is failure only a little flushing will be needed. When the nursing period ends and there are teeth to invite solid food, ***then at your peril feed more than three times daily***. This duly guarded and with never a between-meal taxing, you can let nature have large liberty at a well-spread table.

What about yourself during the nursing period? We will consider at our next meeting.

LECTURE XXV.

IRRIGATIONS FURTHER CONSIDERED IN REPLY TO A QUESTION—FOOD AS AFFECTING THE NATURAL SUPPLY—HERD MILK, SHALL IT BE DILUTED?—LIME-WATER—THE WEANING PERIOD—NATURE'S RECREATIVE DEMANDS DURING THE GROWING YEARS—NATURE IS THE SCHOOL-ROOM—AN ILLUSTRATIVE CASE.

My Friends the Women:

I begin my talk this morning by the consideration of a question. "What will the doctor suggest about medicated irrigations when the discharge is profuse and of bad odor?" This is a very pertinent question, and I am glad to answer it again because of my intense conviction that women are often subjected to annoying, needless, very taxing, overtreatments. They who suffer in this way as a general fact, are already suffering from debility, particularly of the vascular system, and hence they all the more need to be kept free from needless physical exertion.

Now you are to keep in mind what I have already tried to enforce upon you, that the danger-points are the parts abraded by injury and the placental surface, and are the only danger-points. Now, again, let me try to make you see that the instant a part becomes injured, nature begins to generate a protective coat, to construct a line of defense, to build up breastworks; do you not see then, that there is need, of the greatest care that we do not destroy by inundation, our only defense against the arch-enemy, the microbe?

I cannot suggest further than that masses in a state of decomposition may be relieved by irrigation, but that you are to beware how you flood the placental site. In our present state of knowledge as to the conditions behind septic absorption, there are two things beyond dispute—first, that rich blood is easily the first of germicides: second that all abraded spots need the instant and continuous defensive coating that nature always tries to generate and maintain.

There is some advantage in the early days of the lying-in, in posing the body from time to time to have the aid of gravity to relieve when discharges are profuse.

And now what are we to say as to the care of the general health during the nursing year? The first point that naturally arises in my mind because it is in yours, is as to what the diet shall be, as to results upon the maternal supply. It is the very common impression that certain foods and drinks must be taken or avoided, for milk reasons, regardless of what nature's voice may be in the matter. Now all I need to say to you in this matter, since for a whole year you are to eat, digest, assimilate for the sustenance of two lives, is that there can be no period in your lives when you ought to take your every meal with such unction of relish. Can this be done if you fill your stomachs with certain nutrient drinks or foods, supposed to be persuaders of the mammary glands?

No, you will do nothing of the kind; you will guard your stomach as you guard the life of your helpless infant, with direct reference to keeping it in the highest possible state of functional power. You will take unusual care to guard against undue fatigue every day of your lives, and will so cultivate hunger that even as with the wielder of the pick and shovel, you will best relish those foods that will give you the greatest abiding strength for your double need of living.

I am reminded that I have said nothing as to those atrocious enemies of the nursing period, mammary abscesses and ulcered nipples. These are diseases for which you will call in your physician. I will only say that the best time to treat them is before they put in an appearance, and this is, as you well know, by that wiser daily living you are aware of through iteration very often reiterated. These terrible enemies of the nursing period seize upon the weak points of the defensive lines and hence *the need* during all the months of the pregnant life to keep all the lines in the highest possible state of defiance to attack.

I am asked what about diluting milk with water when it has to be used as a substitute for the maternal supply, and whether it is any advantage to add lime-water. Water only adds bulk to the ration; it does not in the least diminish the task, the exhaustive task, of converting herd-green cheese into assimilable nourishment in the delicate stomach of an infant. As for lime-water its first action is to neutralize the action of the natural acid constituent of the gastric juice, and by so much cause the loss of power. Herd-milk must continue for years to come, to take the lead as a substitute for the maternal supply, and the one supreme need is to have it pure and to administer it at exact periods, and with a slowness that will accord with the weakness of the stomach it is to so heavily tax.

One lady with each of her two most delicate babies took the pains to spend from thirty to thirty-five minutes at each of the four daily feedings. By so doing, the stomach had to deal with only minute particles of cheese, and hunger became so toned down that there was rarely any danger of overfeeding. That mother exceeded all the mothers that ever came under my observation for cheerful, patient, persistent devotion to the need as she saw it, and her reward was that before either got half through the first year of life their bodies seemed to have reached the very highest state of physical perfection, and do you believe it, it was only at the rarest intervals that either required any attention at night, and that both were fully able to meet the task of getting to sleep without assistance, any time of night. It is probable that the care of infancy was never reduced nearer to a minimum than it was in these cases after the sixth month.

In one of my families there was the tenth child born in January, and the eleventh in December of the same year. These had only four feedings during twenty-four hours for four months; only three thereafter, the last at 6 P. M. AS for the nights they used them habitually for that sleep that went steadily on without maternal aid. These gave the mother the least trouble of all the living eleven. She had found out, you see, that widely spaced, regular meals did not involve the danger of starving. That was a mother who, doing nearly all the work of homemaking for the family of thirteen, realized every day of her life, the relief that came from not having to prepare wasted meals, and perhaps very few families of such dimensions ever got on with less calls from the family physician.

Now a word as to the weaning period. At about the end of the first year, nature begins to hint of a more varied bill of fare, and very decidedly when the double teeth begin to appear. The meals must now be reduced to three daily with no between-meal indulgences.

You will not get any solid food eaten that is not relished, and you will have to wisely select from what taste will indicate whether of the latest prepared baby-food, or bread, fruit, rice, or blubber, as geography shall determine. What other need I say than this?

I now take up a most interesting subject, the subject of what you shall do with your rollicking families until that period of maturity when the so-called business tastes begin to indicate what the mission in life is to be. The supremest need in child, in youth life is *recreation.* It is the oxygen in the air we breathe, the draught to the flame, in its power to keep the stomach in the highest possible state of functional activity. And this is the need of every hour of the day in the growing period of life. During this period, nature has been so wise as to provide that the happiness of the hour by hour generation, shall be all sufficient; that there shall be no need to recall the happy hours of the past nor any to anticipate happy hours in the days to come. There can be no corroding care to slow down the digestive machinery; in short, to meet all the imperative demands of the body there must be in every moment of existence during the waking hours the very loftiest cheer. Less than this means by so much, a decline in power to fully digest the needed amounts and hence a disease inciting tax on vital power.

What about the arrest of nature in her legitimate duties and the holding in confinement for five days, each six hours long, in a crowded school-room and the worry over text books whose every page is like the face of an enemy? Let me condense an idea so that you shall never forget it; every time you arrest nature in her rollicking gambols, and put her to a hated task, whether over text-books in that same old school-room or even to the slightest of duties that has not pleasure in it, you by so much arrest the due processes of nutrition and, by *so much in-cite processes of disease in parts weak through heredity!!*

With this physiological fact ever in your minds, and a fact beyond human refutation, it will be yours to add all the recreative element possible to all the tasks you shall impose upon child life, upon youth. Away in the far future our school system will be readjusted to this supreme need of the developing years, and in that age brain tasks will have the reinforcement of the recreation that shall come when the page of the text-book shall be as the face of the friend that brings only the most cheery news. It is your supreme duty to your growing children that they shall have that habitual care that shall enable them to reach mature age with the least possible cultivation of hereditary weakness into disease, and with that culture of the moral nature that has nothing of the task in it. There should never be any labor put upon the child, the youth, that is void of the recreative element.

Whatever of worth there shall be in the rollicking child or youth is to be a matter of the development of a germ within, that culture can neither give nor take away. The tastes are inborn, ingrained, and these shall determine whether the happy innocent boy is to become a servant of the cross or a burglar. The Ward School has no power to determine that your boy shall not grow up innocent of books, no matter how many terms he may be compelled to gaze on hated pages with hazy vision; and the lack of ward schools, of High Schools cannot determine that his eager brain shall not become an encyclopedia.

Do I really need to particularize on this subject? I gave you the facts; it is yours alone to use them wisely, and you will use your light wisely, lest through your remissness, you may be called upon to finally gaze upon the face of that delicate boy or of that delicate girl, after the body has been placed in a casket.

Some years ago I was called to see a bright little girl for the special purpose of making her strong enough to habitually walk nearly a mile every morning through storms, snows, sleets, etc., to be imprisoned for six mortal hours per day in a dingy school-room. She was the sole survivor, her two brothers, at an early age, having departed suddenly because of some mystery of the brain. I found exceeding worry, not on account of ailing, but that the fitful attendance was interfering with high marks. I also found the low mutterings, and all the air heavy and dark with an impending storm that might at any moment as a hurricane burst among brain centers. What, standing in such a storm center, was my duty to the parents who lived, moved and breathed only for this lone survivor?

"Your daughter must never enter a school-room again with her text-book in hand; henceforward, you must be content with only physical and moral culture, until she reaches an age where the pages of the text-book shall be like the faces of friends, or an act on the stage. This is a case not of mental culture, but of a life, or a death that **may** come as the bolt from the clouds." My words reached the brain centers to which they were driven, and a delicate girl was permitted to develop into a bright womanhood, with a keenly alert mind that met all other minds in social life with the most astonishing ease and fluency of speech, and a charming thoughtlessness of the lack of textbook reserves. True, when the joys of mastered Latin, or zoology, or botany were revealed with sparkling eyes and burning words by her cultured friends, then there may have been a passing emotion of subdued regret, and a recalling with infinite depths of feeling that

"Of all sad words of tongue or pen,
The saddest are these, it might have been."

Said a boy soldier, riding on the caisson of a battery that was being withdrawn for repairs on the first day of Gettysburg, "General Reynolds is dead, I would rather be a live private any day than a dead general."

The doting parents still have a live daughter who has never had any need or care to teach, and strange to say she never seems to reveal any culture deficiency as measured by the standard of her friend graduates, except when the joys of mastered text-books are being revealed to her.

We shall meet just once more to consider mental culture in its relations to disease culture, and to give you some parting admonitions.

LECTURE XXVI.

THE SCHOOLS AND DESEASE CULTURE—A CASE—ILLUSTRAIVE AU-
TOBIOGRAPHY—CLOSING ADMONITION.

My Friends the Women:

It does not come within the scope of my morning lectures to consider mental culture except incidentally, in its relation to disease culture. It is my conception that the Ward Schools are hot-beds of mental worry and not of mental culture; that they are centers of a barbaric war against the natural forces of mental and physical growth, and therefore against life itself. Have I any reason for this radical conception? Let us consider.

Since, as I have before told you, recreation is to digestion what the breeze is to the flame, the child, the young mind needs this life force during every awakened moment as the lungs need fresh air.

School law, with its heavy, iron hand, invades our homes, seizes upon our innocents, drags them to prison where they must languish during six hours of five days of every week, leaving only one day per week for recreation, and this for seven, eight or nine months of those years most vitally important for healthy development. It cannot be denied by any who have an intelligent conception of the origin and development of disease, that every hour, every moment, spent in irksome confinement in the heavy, fixed, vitiated air of the school-room, worrying over textbooks whose pages are as the face of an enemy, is an hour, where disease culture is going insidiously on.

As you are all aware, there is no time for play in the morning, and little at noon, and not much in the evening, and Sunday is a day of austere rest, of restraint laid upon brain and muscle. And to what end is this war against nature, these long years of sinning in the sight of heaven against innocent childhood and youth? Does there exist a mortal man or woman who has become learned through much schooling who does not date the beginning of the real educative process at that period when the page of the text-book becomes as the face of a friend, and the school-room as recreative as the school yard, or college campus?

In the city of my home there are eight hundred hapless boys enduring the disease-inciting attrition of the Ward Schools because of the iron hand of law. Eight hundred boys in the ward schools; eight in the graduating class of the high school on the average. The rest fall out by the way, because Nature is stronger than law and the ambition of parents, and about all they will have acquired during their weeks, months and years of imprisonment that they will not easily forget is ability to read and write and something of the simpler mathematics. These are the proportions, these the achievements, and only law will ever change them. Behind all human effort is a want, whether it is money from the exploded safe or that which comes from labor in the jungles to give light where there is only darkness. Want is the motive power behind all our doing, and heredity determines largely what it shall be. Your poets, painters, scientists, musicians, artisans, wielders of pick and shovel, neat, orderly, provident housekeepers are born; they are never bred in the schools nor in your homes. Heredity determines that one of your sons shall be a spendthrift and the other a miser, and Nature will not reverse her plan through any culture, no matter how enforced.

Is there not a frightful per cent, of men who grew up in the most cultured of homes, under the best of moral and intellectual training, who are now laboring six days in every week with cropped heads and striped clothes? Success in life, no matter what the avocation, must have, does have, want as the motive power. Nature will have her own ways very largely as to what the doing shall be to satisfy the daily wants, whether those ways are along the paths of virtue or of vice, and they are not the ways of the ward schools, nor of any schools during the growing age. "But," says one, "will you abolish our ward schools?" No, not the schools, but everything in the schools that deprives both teacher and pupils of the heaven-born right of so living and doing that their bodies may be kept in the best possible conditions of defense against disease. There should be neither teaching nor study that worries the mind. Six hours per day in the hopeless labor of trying to raise the marks above Nature's easy reaching needs eighteen hours of recreative repose for all of life-forces, and for your sons and daughters the largest liberty to regain the lost balance.

Since every hour spent in irksome confinement is an hour of disease-culture, and law has willed that there must be only one day in the week during eight or nine months in the year for disease-defying growth, what are you to do when your little kingdoms of heaven are suffering such violence because the violent are taking them by force? Let me give you an illustrative answer.

An anxious mother came to me recently whose delicate daughter is a grievous sufferer from profuse periods. There have been the mornings of unrelished breakfasts; the walks of nearly a mile to and from the hurried dinners; the evening meals taken with all the powers crying aloud from exhaustion, but only as a preliminary to more study.

Since there is a towering ambition for the graduating day, it is advised that this girl have a general meal soon after returning from the afternoon session, and that from thence until the next morning there shall be no worrying over text-books. This meal will be light enough to permit a clearing of the stomach before an early bedtime. On arising in the morning there will be an hour of the best possible condition for study; a walk to the school will freshen all the faculties, and then by reason of an empty stomach there will be the best possible conditions of ***perception, comprehension*** and ***retention.*** The noon hour and a half will be devoted to rest and the digestion of the lightest of luncheons which will be well handled by reason of those long hours, without digestive worry, and the work will not cause very much mental sluggishness; hence three more hours of study with only slightly impaired conditions. By so ordering the living and study habits there will be the highest average of marks, with the lowest average of disease culture, and with a strong probability of reaching the graduating day with something left of constitutional power.

Since the amount of general muscle exercise is diminished a good deal more than one-half during those worrying days of school life, the eating must be cut down to be more in accord with the actual need; and the line of care devised for this delicate miss applies with equal force to *every* pupil in *every* school. By so ordering the living habits of all daughters during the critical, the maturing years, all the more critical because so much of life has to be endured in fixed air and darkened rooms, there will be the highest possible reach of sustained health.

Later, perhaps in the afternoon of time, when school, law has become more nearly adjusted to physiological law, the morning session of the ward school will begin at eight o'clock with every pupil ready for the assigned duties with a clear head and an empty stomach. At ten o'clock the session will close, when on reaching home, there will be in due readiness the first meal of the day, which will be taken without any nervous haste, for there are to be four hours of recreative, digestive stimulation. At two o'clock they will have their stomachs so cleared and their minds and bodies so rested and refreshed that there will be two hours more of the best possible conditions for mental culture. At four o'clock the study of the day is ended, and on reaching the homes they all will be ready for another general meal which will be taken early enough to give the stomach time to complete its task before the eyes close in sleep.

With the meals so regulated and the hours of confinement in the school-room so cut down there will be the largest possible average of mental culture and the least of disease culture. In that golden age of schools there will be no teaching that will impoverish body, soul and mind; because next to being qualified to teach, it will be required that there will be health to teach, and so law, body, soul and mind will be in harmony. There is nothing like the sunshine of perfect health, and nowhere is it more needed than in rooms where young souls are wilting for want of air and light.

In that golden age the teacher's chair will be a throne where there will be health power in reserve, and only they shall fill it who have the divine right which health can give. And the home will be enlarged and brightened because the mothers will not be living sacrifices to the tyranny of the school-room! They will have very much more of the society of their daughters, much more of the helpful aid of those daughters which will be a culture to them of practical value far beyond anything derived from text books. The daughters of that time to come will all have something of that general muscular activity that is involved in home service during term-time; but all cultures will be subordinate to health culture. "Health is the first wealth," says Emerson.

Need I enlarge on the health and care those sons and daughters require during the maturing years when there is a rapid emergence into height and breath without strength? Those are the years when there are the largest liabilities, possibilities of disease culture, and therefore it must be yours to see that their living habits are in such habitual accord with nature that their ambushed enemies' hereditary weakness, shall not become subjected to an insidious development.

My friends, let me give you a final illustration from life in a suggestive parallel. I was "born and bred" in a large country home. The boys of my time never wore boots, hence damp or wet feet during the rains and snow of winter, and often intense suffering from cold feet; they never wore underclothes nor overcoats, hence often severe suffering in the coldest weather. There were no warmed bedrooms except the one hard by the kitchen fire, hence there could be no sleep in the cold season until shivering, shrinking bodies had thawed out ice-cold sheets.

The oldest son in a large family, my services were of the first importance, and accordingly manual labor far heavier than my years and strength would warrant, was unwittingly and habitually thrust upon me. From my grandfather I was the luckless inheritor of a weak stomach that eating never satisfied, hence, always hungry, my stomach was kept always full except when there was a sudden emptying through an indignant righteous upheaval. In due time through eating habits that were daily outrages of all digestive conditions, my winters became involved with a series of colds, with headaches and bilious attacks thrown in for variety. Finally while yet in my early teens I became the victim of that outrageous so-called disease "nervous dyspepsia."

To the medical science of the time, to the medical science of to-day, this was and is a disease, whose multiform symptoms then needed, as at the present, multiform treatment. There was no conception that all the trouble arose from avoidable abuse of the stomach, for which remedial treatments were as void of sense, of science as they always were and always will be, futile in desired results.

The wreckage went on; "The old man of the sea" was upon my back and my life forces were withering under his relentless grasp. I was borne down to the deepest depths from which to emerge as one back from the dead, and under such heavy bonds to my stomach that like Bunyan of old I have to go "in chains to preach to them in chains," to persuade them to beware of the terrors, the tortures of transgressed law.

There are three sons in my house whose daily living habits have been the objects of that more enlightened care born of suffering long endured. There has been no taxing labor; no suffering from frozen feet; no shivering in frosted beds. For ten years there has been no eating without natural hunger; ten years almost entirely free from colds and never severe ones. Ten years without headaches or billious attacks and no ailings not clearly traceable to avoidable cause.

Thus have I tried to guard their lives against their unknown enemies, the *insidious, hereditary, impossibilities of disease,* and thus have I tried to raise those lives to such a luxury of daily food, such a luxury of between meal comfort, that any and all drinks of the alcoholics will cause, not exhilaration, but mental and physical depression. The best has no superlative. Alcoholics have no tempting power over a perfectly nourished body.

My friends, ignorance of the ways and means of disease culture is all abounding, and so dense, so void of the least ray of intelligence as to be nothing less than *terrible*.

Two centuries or more ago a bright young girl in her later teens left a home where "the parents were counted godly" and with young love's simple, burning, unquestioning faith, became the wife of a young man who, according to his after estimate, was one of the chiefest of all living sinners. She took with her as her marriage portion an unpretentious little book called, "The plain man's pathway to Heaven." It attracted the interest of one of the brightest minds the world ever saw, and a seed was planted in a soul that became the greatest religious genius of any age, and lo the Pilgrim's Progress is the harvest!

These morning lectures have been delivered to you with conviction at a white heat, and with no thought of the use of language but to make you see Nature as she appears to my vision; and they are intended to constitute a very plain pathway to even the plainest of women, a pathway straight, narrow, with no side tracks nor branches that do not lead to despair; a pathway that leads only to the "Delectable Mountains," whose other name is the ***best attainable health.***

Some of you have sons and daughters who are soon to rend your family circles, leaving behind vacant chairs, torn-apart nerves and quivering wounds that time will never heal. They are going into the dense darkness of darkest Africa to spend their lives in jungles, far beyond the reach of medical advice and care, that the world may sing,

"The morning light is breaking,
The darkness disappears."

Will it not be well for them as they go down into the depths to become deeply imbued with the "New Gospel of Health"; well that they shall know that only Nature heals the sick; well, even vitally important, that they shall know that it is a gospel that applies to every human ailing as the Gospel of Jesus Christ applies to every moral need; well for them to know that the more climatic, dietetic and social conditions are adverse to health, go is the need to live in closer walk with God according to laws "manifest in the flesh"? Let them go forth with the largest faith, born of culture, that Nature is the great physician, with only the rarest need of remedies; let them go down into the depths with the very largest faith that the "New Gospel of Health" applies with all the more force, as debility, age, disease, have so weakened constitutional power: with all the more force, where the breath of life has to be drawn from air dense with malaria, where hearts must beat with painful throbs because home, country and kindred have been given up, and where all of Life's forces are heavily laden because so much has to be endured through privation.

Let them have the clearest possible conception, that, the highest constitutional degree of health can be maintained, whether existence be upon the "Delectable Mountains," or amid the "pestilence that walketh in darkness," or "the destruction that wasteth at noonday," *only by the very largest compliance with the moral, the mental and the chemical conditions involved in the conversion of food into living, moving, breathing, thinking tissue.*

And you my friends, the women, henceforward, during all the days of your lives to be home missionaries, go you forth also to make your light shine in all the dark places, that life that now is, may be brought into more and more harmony with that perfect life that is to come.

THE END.

The Codes Of Hammurabi And Moses
W. W. Davies

QTY

The discovery of the Hammurabi Code is one of the greatest achievements of archaeology, and is of paramount interest, not only to the student of the Bible, but also to all those interested in ancient history...

Religion   **ISBN:** *1-59462-338-4*   **Pages:132**
MSRP $12.95

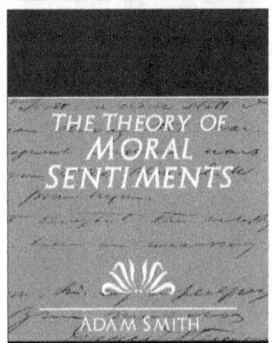

The Theory of Moral Sentiments
Adam Smith

QTY

This work from 1749. contains original theories of conscience amd moral judgment and it is the foundation for systemof morals.

Philosophy   **ISBN:** *1-59462-777-0*   **Pages:536**
MSRP $19.95

Jessica's First Prayer
Hesba Stretton

QTY

In a screened and secluded corner of one of the many railway-bridges which span the streets of London there could be seen a few years ago, from five o'clock every morning until half past eight, a tidily set-out coffee-stall, consisting of a trestle and board, upon which stood two large tin cans, with a small fire of charcoal burning under each so as to keep the coffee boiling during the early hours of the morning when the work-people were thronging into the city on their way to their daily toil...

Pages:84

Childrens   **ISBN:** *1-59462-373-2*   *MSRP $9.95*

My Life and Work
Henry Ford

QTY

Henry Ford revolutionized the world with his implementation of mass production for the Model T automobile. Gain valuable business insight into his life and work with his own auto-biography... "We have only started on our development of our country we have not as yet, with all our talk of wonderful progress, done more than scratch the surface. The progress has been wonderful enough but..."

Pages:300

Biographies/   **ISBN:** *1-59462-198-5*   *MSRP $21.95*

The Art of Cross-Examination
Francis Wellman

QTY

I presume it is the experience of every author, after his first book is published upon an important subject, to be almost overwhelmed with a wealth of ideas and illustrations which could readily have been included in his book, and which to his own mind, at least, seem to make a second edition inevitable. Such certainly was the case with me; and when the first edition had reached its sixth impression in five months, I rejoiced to learn that it seemed to my publishers that the book had met with a sufficiently favorable reception to justify a second and considerably enlarged edition. ..

Reference   ISBN: *1-59462-647-2*

Pages:412

MSRP $19.95

On the Duty of Civil Disobedience
Henry David Thoreau

QTY

Thoreau wrote his famous essay, On the Duty of Civil Disobedience, as a protest against an unjust but popular war and the immoral but popular institution of slave-owning. He did more than write—he declined to pay his taxes, and was hauled off to gaol in consequence. Who can say how much this refusal of his hastened the end of the war and of slavery ?

Law   ISBN: *1-59462-747-9*

Pages:48

MSRP $7.45

Dream Psychology Psychoanalysis for Beginners
Sigmund Freud

QTY

Sigmund Freud, born Sigismund Schlomo Freud (May 6, 1856 - September 23, 1939), was a Jewish-Austrian neurologist and psychiatrist who co-founded the psychoanalytic school of psychology. Freud is best known for his theories of the unconscious mind, especially involving the mechanism of repression; his redefinition of sexual desire as mobile and directed towards a wide variety of objects; and his therapeutic techniques, especially his understanding of transference in the therapeutic relationship and the presumed value of dreams as sources of insight into unconscious desires.

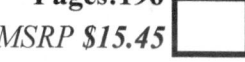

Psychology   ISBN: *1-59462-905-6*

Pages:196

MSRP $15.45

the miracle of right thought
Orison Swett Marden

QTY

Believe with all of your heart that you will do what you were made to do. When the mind has once formed the habit of holding cheerful, happy, prosperous pictures, it will not be easy to form the opposite habit. It does not matter how improbable or how far away this realization may see, or how dark the prospects may be, if we visualize them as best we can, as vividly as possible, hold tenaciously to them and vigorously struggle to attain them, they will gradually become actualized, realized in the life. But a desire, a longing without endeavor, a yearning abandoned or held indifferently will vanish without realization.

Pages:360

Self Help   ISBN: *1-59462-644-8*

MSRP $25.45

QTY

The Rosicrucian Cosmo-Conception Mystic Christianity *by Max Heindel*   ISBN: *1-59462-188-8*   **$38.95**
The Rosicrucian Cosmo-conception is not dogmatic, neither does it appeal to any other authority than the reason of the student. It is: not controversial, but is: sent forth in the, hope that it may help to clear...   New Age/Religion Pages 646

Abandonment To Divine Providence *by Jean-Pierre de Caussade*   ISBN: *1-59462-228-0*   **$25.95**
"The Rev. Jean Pierre de Caussade was one of the most remarkable spiritual writers of the Society of Jesus in France in the 18th Century. His death took place at Toulouse in 1751. His works have gone through many editions and have been republished...   Inspirational/Religion Pages 400

Mental Chemistry *by Charles Haanel*   ISBN: *1-59462-192-6*   **$23.95**
Mental Chemistry allows the change of material conditions by combining and appropriately utilizing the power of the mind. Much like applied chemistry creates something new and unique out of careful combinations of chemicals the mastery of mental chemistry...   New Age Pages 354

The Letters of Robert Browning and Elizabeth Barret Barrett 1845-1846 vol II   ISBN: *1-59462-193-4*   **$35.95**
by Robert Browning and Elizabeth Barrett   Biographies Pages 596

Gleanings In Genesis (volume I) *by Arthur W. Pink*   ISBN: *1-59462-130-6*   **$27.45**
Appropriately has Genesis been termed "the seed plot of the Bible" for in it we have, in germ form, almost all of the great doctrines which are afterwards fully developed in the books of Scripture which follow...   Religion/Inspirational Pages 420

The Master Key *by L. W. de Laurence*   ISBN: *1-59462-001-6*   **$30.95**
In no branch of human knowledge has there been a more lively increase of the spirit of research during the past few years than in the study of Psychology, Concentration and Mental Discipline. The requests for authentic lessons in Thought Control, Mental Discipline and...   New Age/Business Pages 422

The Lesser Key Of Solomon Goetia *by L. W. de Laurence*   ISBN: *1-59462-092-X*   **$9.95**
This translation of the first book of the "Lemegton" which is now for the first time made accessible to students of Talismanic Magic was done, after careful collation and edition, from numerous Ancient Manuscripts in Hebrew, Latin, and French...   New Age/Occult Pages 92

Rubaiyat Of Omar Khayyam *by Edward Fitzgerald*   ISBN:*1-59462-332-5*   **$13.95**
Edward Fitzgerald, whom the world has already learned, in spite of his own efforts to remain within the shadow of anonymity, to look upon as one of the rarest poets of the century, was born at Bredfield, in Suffolk, on the 31st of March, 1809. He was the third son of John Purcell...   Music Pages 172

Ancient Law *by Henry Maine*   ISBN: *1-59462-128-4*   **$29.95**
The chief object of the following pages is to indicate some of the earliest ideas of mankind, as they are reflected in Ancient Law, and to point out the relation of those ideas to modern thought.   Religion/History Pages 452

Far-Away Stories *by William J. Locke*   ISBN: *1-59462-129-2*   **$19.45**
"Good wine needs no bush, but a collection of mixed vintages does. And this book is just such a collection. Some of the stories I do not want to remain buried for ever in the museum files of dead magazine-numbers an author's not unpardonable vanity..."   Fiction Pages 272

Life of David Crockett *by David Crockett*   ISBN: *1-59462-250-7*   **$27.45**
"Colonel David Crockett was one of the most remarkable men of the times in which he lived. Born in humble life, but gifted with a strong will, an indomitable courage, and unremitting perseverance...   Biographies/New Age Pages 424

Lip-Reading *by Edward Nitchie*   ISBN: *1-59462-206-X*   **$25.95**
Edward B. Nitchie, founder of the New York School for the Hard of Hearing, now the Nitchie School of Lip-Reading, Inc, wrote "LIP-READING Principles and Practice". The development and perfecting of this meritorious work on lip-reading was an undertaking...   How-to Pages 400

A Handbook of Suggestive Therapeutics, Applied Hypnotism, Psychic Science   ISBN: *1-59462-214-0*   **$24.95**
by Henry Munro   Health/New Age/Health/Self-help Pages 376

A Doll's House: and Two Other Plays *by Henrik Ibsen*   ISBN: *1-59462-112-8*   **$19.95**
Henrik Ibsen created this classic when in revolutionary 1848 Rome. Introducing some striking concepts in playwriting for the realist genre, this play has been studied the world over.   Fiction/Classics/Plays 308

The Light of Asia *by sir Edwin Arnold*   ISBN: *1-59462-204-3*   **$13.95**
In this poetic masterpiece, Edwin Arnold describes the life and teachings of Buddha. The man who was to become known as Buddha to the world was born as Prince Gautama of India but he rejected the worldly riches and abandoned the reigns of power when...   Religion/History/Biographies Pages 170

The Complete Works of Guy de Maupassant *by Guy de Maupassant*   ISBN: *1-59462-157-8*   **$16.95**
"For days and days, nights and nights, I had dreamed of that first kiss which was to consecrate our engagement, and I knew not on what spot I should put my lips..."   Fiction/Classics Pages 240

The Art of Cross-Examination *by Francis L. Wellman*   ISBN: *1-59462-309-0*   **$26.95**
Written by a renowned trial lawyer, Wellman imparts his experience and uses case studies to explain how to use psychology to extract desired information through questioning.   How-to/Science/Reference Pages 408

Answered or Unanswered? *by Louisa Vaughan*   ISBN: *1-59462-248-5*   **$10.95**
Miracles of Faith in China   Religion Pages 112

The Edinburgh Lectures on Mental Science (1909) *by Thomas*   ISBN: *1-59462-008-3*   **$11.95**
This book contains the substance of a course of lectures recently given by the writer in the Queen Street Hall, Edinburgh. Its purpose is to indicate the Natural Principles governing the relation between Mental Action and Material Conditions...   New Age/Psychology Pages 148

Ayesha *by H. Rider Haggard*   ISBN: *1-59462-301-5*   **$24.95**
Verily and indeed it is the unexpected that happens! Probably if there was one person upon the earth from whom the Editor of this, and of a certain previous history, did not expect to hear again...   Classics Pages 380

Ayala's Angel *by Anthony Trollope*   ISBN: *1-59462-352-X*   **$29.95**
The two girls were both pretty, but Lucy who was twenty-one who supposed to be simple and comparatively unattractive, whereas Ayala was credited, as her Bombwhat romantic name might show, with poetic charm and a taste for romance. Ayala when her father died was nineteen...   Fiction Pages 484

The American Commonwealth *by James Bryce*   ISBN: *1-59462-286-8*   **$34.45**
An interpretation of American democratic political theory. It examines political mechanics and society from the perspective of Scotsman James Bryce   Politics Pages 572

Stories of the Pilgrims *by Margaret P. Pumphrey*   ISBN: *1-59462-116-0*   **$17.95**
This book explores pilgrims religious oppression in England as well as their escape to Holland and eventual crossing to America on the Mayflower, and their early days in New England...   History Pages 268

QTY

The Fasting Cure *by Sinclair Upton*
ISBN: *1-59462-222-1* **$13.95**

In the Cosmopolitan Magazine for May, 1910, and in the Contemporary Review (London) for April, 1910, I published an article dealing with my experiences in fasting. I have written a great many magazine articles, but never one which attracted so much attention... New Age/Self Help/Health Pages 164

Hebrew Astrology *by Sepharial*
ISBN: *1-59462-308-2* **$13.45**

In these days of advanced thinking it is a matter of common observation that we have left many of the old landmarks behind and that we are now pressing forward to greater heights and to a wider horizon than that which represented the mind-content of our progenitors... Astrology Pages 144

Thought Vibration or The Law of Attraction in the Thought World
ISBN: *1-59462-127-6* **$12.95**

by William Walker Atkinson
Psychology/Religion Pages 144

Optimism *by Helen Keller*
ISBN: *1-59462-108-X* **$15.95**

Helen Keller was blind, deaf, and mute since 19 months old, yet famously learned how to overcome these handicaps, communicate with the world, and spread her lectures promoting optimism. An inspiring read for everyone... Biographies/Inspirational Pages 84

Sara Crewe *by Frances Burnett*
ISBN: *1-59462-360-0* **$9.45**

In the first place, Miss Minchin lived in London. Her home was a large, dull, tall one, in a large, dull square, where all the houses were alike, and all the sparrows were alike, and where all the door-knockers made the same heavy sound... Childrens/Classic Pages 88

The Autobiography of Benjamin Franklin *by Benjamin Franklin*
ISBN: *1-59462-135-7* **$24.95**

The Autobiography of Benjamin Franklin has probably been more extensively read than any other American historical work, and no other book of its kind has had such ups and downs of fortune. Franklin lived for many years in England, where he was agent... Biographies/History Pages 332

Name	
Email	
Telephone	
Address	
City, State ZIP	

☐ **Credit Card**   ☐ **Check / Money Order**

Credit Card Number	
Expiration Date	
Signature	

Please Mail to: Book Jungle
PO Box 2226
Champaign, IL 61825
or Fax to: 630-214-0564

ORDERING INFORMATION

web: *www.bookjungle.com*
email: *sales@bookjungle.com*
fax: *630-214-0564*
mail: *Book Jungle PO Box 2226 Champaign, IL 61825*
or PayPal *to sales@bookjungle.com*

Please contact us for bulk discounts

DIRECT-ORDER TERMS

**20% Discount if You Order
Two or More Books**
Free Domestic Shipping!
Accepted: Master Card, Visa,
Discover, American Express